I0712805

HIDING LIONS INSIDE LAMBS...

THE
FORTRESS
AND THE
FIGURINE

BRANDI ELISE SZEKER

<u>**The Pawn and The Puppet Series**</u>
The Pawn and The Puppet
The Master and The Marionette
The Puppeteer and the Poisoned Pawn
The Doll and The Domination
The Fortress and The Figurine (novella)
The Clock and The Carnival

Content Warning:

Disclaimer: This book contains explicit content and dark elements and may be considered offensive to some readers. Check trigger warnings before reading. It is not intended for anyone under 18 years of age. Please store your files wisely, where they cannot be accessed by underage readers.

Triggers: Accessibility issues, emotional distress, infantilization, loss of independence and dignity, suicidal thoughts, bullying, traumatic flashbacks, torture, depression, gore, sexism, eating disorder, mention of animal cruelty (off page), animal death, disturbing imagery, graphic violence and gore, sexism and misogyny, self-deprecating language or negative self-talk, mention of kidnapping, mental health issues sexually explicit content and kinks.

Do not continue if you are unsure of the contents of this book.

*To the reader suffering
from a disability.
You deserve a crown, a kingdom,
and a morally gray warrior
with a huge shlong,
on their knees to please.*

Keep going.

"What is to give light must endure burning."
-Viktor E. Frankel

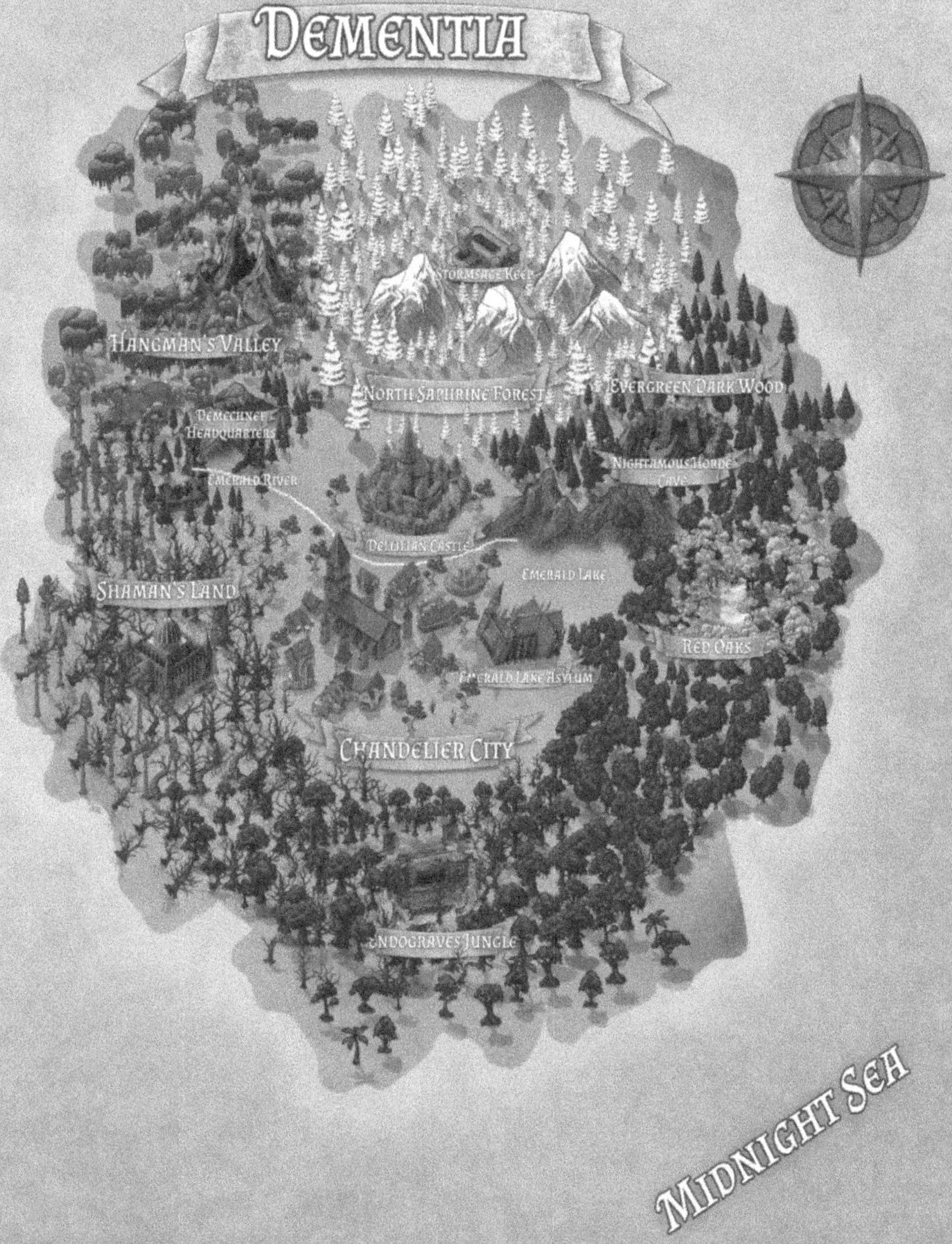

Dementia
Stormsage Keep
Hangman's Valley
North Saphrine Forest
Evergreen Dark Wood
Demechnet Headquarters
Nightfamous Horde Cave
Emerald River
Delilian Castle
Emerald Lake
Shaman's Land
Red Oaks
Emerald Lake Asylum
Chandelier City
Endograves Jungle
Midnight Sea

Author's Note

Someone very close to me recently lost their ability to walk after a brutal accident. This happened during the pandemic. They had to recover in a hospital for several months without seeing family or friends, without a hug, without affection. It nearly killed us all to watch helplessly. Their journey has moved me, brought me closer to God.

Writing Ruth's story brought me back to those days. And I've never known a greater respect than for anyone who has suffered something similar.

After reading this novella, I ask that my readers seek to educate themselves on disabilities and ableism. Though this is a work of fiction, I hope it will open your eyes to different ways of life and appreciation for those struggling on different journeys than you.

If you are suffering, know that we're with you. The characters in these books are with you. My readers are with you. I am with you.

Playlist

Butterflies by Tom Odell, AURORA
Dead Man by David Kushner
Skin and Bones by David Kushner
Carolina by Taylor Swift
Can't Catch Me Now by Olivia Rodrigo
Snow on The Beach by Taylor Swift, Lana Del Rey
Flying by James Newton Howard
Kingdom Dance by Alan Menken
You Failed Me Finn by James Newton Howard
White Hart by James Newton Howard
Cold by Aqualung, Lucy Schwartz
Carry You Home by Alex Warren
My Tears Ricochet by Taylor Swift
Heal by Tom Odell

The playlist can be found on Spotify by searching for "The Fortress and The Figurine"

1. Of Burdens and Beds

Ruth

The sheets are warm and sopping wet.

I can hear the daunting *drip, drip, drip* as it leaks from the cheap spring mattress onto the tile floor. My thighs throb and ache from infection. And it doesn't help that I'm trying to sleep on soaking sheets.

I've wet the bed.

Please, God. No.

I squeeze my eyes shut against the blaring moonlight through the infirmary window. And for a few seconds, I lie perfectly still and pretend I lose control of my bladder in my sleep. The nightmare of being left in the prison to rot came back like a tidal wave sweeping me under its deadly collapse. And like clockwork, the mattress is drenched, and I'm lying in my own urine helplessly. I can't get up and clean my own mess. I can't do *anything*.

To make matters worse, Warrose is sleeping three feet from me.

He never leaves.

For a while, he fought the nurses to stay in my room even though his back looked like a slab of raw, carved-up meat. But he agreed to get medical attention if they did it in my room.

Drip, drip, drip.

The hyperventilating starts without warning.

Drip, drip, drip.

Have I not endured enough? The constant pain? The endless, gory nightmares? Must I also fall victim to wetting the bed in front of the man I'm attracted to?

I try to breathe quietly through my nose, but am slammed with the grueling scent of urine, sweat, cleaning solvents, and infection.

"Ruth?" Warrose's sleepy voice is hoarse and deep. "Are you awake?"

If I wasn't a statue before, I certainly am now.

His cot creaks as he sits upright.

Drip, drip, drip.

I hold my breath but can't contain the shivering that rumbles up my thighs and arms. *Please, go back to sleep. Please, don't come to check on me.*

Those heavy footsteps collide with the floor as he takes three strides to my bed. I can smell how close he is as his mountainous frame hovers over me. Campfires and spice. I can sense his eyebrows pulling together in concern. His calloused hand touches the top of my damp forehead as he checks to see if my fever has gotten worse. Another infection. Another scare of me dying in the middle of the night.

Drip, drip, drip.

Warrose goes still at the sound. His giant hand lifts from my face and begins patting the bed to investigate. My stomach curls in on itself as he hits the source of my shame, manifesting into a small death poisoning my insides.

He checks the bandages on my legs to make sure it's not blood.

"Ruth?"

Pity.

That's *pity* in his tone.

He feels fucking terrible. Poor, sad, useless Ruth. The sympathy wrinkles his voice into something strained and choked up.

"Ruth? I'm going to get you out of bed." Warrose tries to slip his hands under me, but my resolve snaps like a dried, dead twig.

"Just. Get. The. Nurse." Venom. Bite. Ice. Spite.

Get out. Get out. Get out!

My dignity is gone. Shriveled. How can I be a woman around him like this? How can I maintain even the slightest bit of confidence as I lie in my own piss? Tears bulge from the corners of my eyes as I glare at his ruggedly gorgeous face in the darkness.

"Now," I order through my teeth. *Please go. Please, don't come back.*

I know how hard this is for him. His style is giving me tough love, fighting to break past my stubbornness no matter the situation. But since we got back to the Chandelier City, and they checked me into this infirmary…

His will to fight and argue has seemed to dissolve after watching me cry myself to sleep, become ill from infections, and have clear signs of suicide ideation.

This has broken him down too.

Warrose pauses with a look of patience. "Okay, little rebel."

I'm propped up on a Sunday morning, clutching a rusted pail to my chest and spewing yellowish-green bile until it sears my esophagus.

Thank God Warrose has left to get me softer, thicker blankets from Marilynn's house. I've been shivering like a newborn left in the snow to die. After another infection, I'm certain this is going to be the duration of my life. Antibiotics. Fever. Chills. Vomiting and nausea. An endless course of medications. Fevered nightmares. Cold sweat. Diarrhea, dizziness, rashes on my backside, self-loathing, crying fits, and a deep longing to get out of this bed and run again.

"So, you're what everyone keeps fussing about."

I open my eyes through the vomit-induced tears and lift my head out of the pail swishing with my puke.

A short, scrawny woman stands in front of my bed with a cane. She wears a fluffy white robe and a matching bathroom towel around her head. Through the blurriness of my vision, her face is that of a skeleton. Gaunt, tired, and so pale her blue veins radiate along her neck.

"What?" is all I can say before I heave again. My tongue burns from the lingering stomach acid.

"This infirmary never gets fatal injuries. My case is normally the worst they get around here." She eyes my bed like a hunting wolf.

I give her a slow blink.

"I faint often and am sick all the time. They give me whatever medication I ask for because I'm an Emerald Wife, an upstanding lady-doll regimen example to society. And a regular patient here."

Ah. I glance over her frail gray hands. *That checks out.*

She pats the bed where my feet should be and snorts. "The rumors were true. Where did your legs run off to, little girl?"

A sweltering anger pulses through my forehead in a thin sheen of sweat.

"I lost them."

"I see that," she says mockingly without blinking. "Are they under your bed?"

The small woman lifts my bed sheets to look under the wire frame.

"No, not here." She smiles with wicked amusement.

I stare at her until my eyes sting, then go bone-dry.

"I'd bet my gorgeous mansion on the hill that you're basking in the profound attention you're receiving from all of those sweet, worried nurses who flood through your room at all hours, hmm?"

What do I have to do to get her the fuck out of my room?

She laughs, then quickly smooths out any smile lines on her face.

"I'm in the room across the hall and seem to be chopped liver since you arrived."

"Are you going to cry about it, or do you just intend to bore me to death?" I finally say through my teeth.

Her eyebrows raise briefly, then she rubs those lines away as well.

"I don't think I've introduced myself." She walks around to my left side with her cane.

"I don't think I care," I respond.

She snorts again. An ugly, bitter sound.

"My name is Apple May." She snatches my vomit pail away from my feeble grip and dumps it over my chest.

2. The New Demechnef Reign

Marilynn

I'm given the Demechnef flag to place on his casket.

The field is filled with soldiers, oligarchs, and anyone who knew of Aurick's real identity. But the only person who's here for me is Niles.

"Take your time. Everyone can wait," he says in my ear.

I told him he didn't need to come to this. I know what the Demechnef's have done to my friends. To his family. I know of the moments that will stain history in blood and trauma that Aurick and Vlademur will pay for in the afterlife. But attending this funeral wasn't even worth a moment of hesitation for Niles. He found a black suit and tie. He styled his hair. He made sure I ate before we left.

To the slow whine of a violin, I approach his outrageously expensive oak box covered in red roses. The flag leaves my fingertips, delicately being set on the center of the glossy wood.

"I'll take good care of our son, Aur. And even though I know how history will write your name, I'll make sure he also hears of your good deeds too." Emotion runs like thick syrup down my throat at the though of him lying in this casket all alone. "You can sleep now."

I didn't think I'd cry. Truthfully, I wondered if I'd be desensitized to it all. But walking away from this glorified grave, I raise my eyes to meet Niles.

And…he's holding his arms out to me.

A flooding sensation burns the backs of my eyes, and his sweet glowing skin becomes a little blurry. Despite the time we shared in the prison, the mark of trauma we now both carry in our hearts, I still have the buried urge to pull away from him.

But not right now.

As we're surrounded by strangers, by the hierarchy of this society, all I really want is a Niles hug.

"Come here, sweetheart," Niles coos as I walk into his chest.

His arms react instantly, curling around my upper body as I press my face into his sternum. The sob I'm clutching for dear life sends a rattle through my lungs, making my back quiver under the tension. He holds me tight and snug, placing the sweetest kisses on the top of my head.

I have always had mixed feelings regarding Aurick Demechnef. Despite his shortcomings, I did fall in love with him at one point in my life, yes. I'm reminded of the long afternoons we'd lie in his backyard garden on a bedsheet, making love, eating ice cream, and talking for hours. There were many times I thought I would slip up and trust him enough to spill the secrets of the sacred prophecy. I never did, because that love turned into disdain when I'd hear him speak to his father, Vlademur, and they would speak fondly of their test subjects— Skylenna and Dessin.

I grew to detest his eagerness to please his abusive father even though he secretly hated him too. And after a while, I became repulsed by their family altogether.

But that doesn't mean that seeing his casket, remembering how he died, how we fell in love…doesn't shatter my heart completely.

It does.

I take a deep inhale of his special aroma. The trademark Niles scent of soap, sunshine, and a little bit of amber from the cologne he insisted on Chekiss buying for him yesterday.

"Are you smelling me again?"

"Shut up," I grumble against his suit jacket.

Niles's chuckle vibrates my cheek. "I told Chekiss this cologne was an aphrodisiac. He literally didn't believe me."

I grin with tears ruining my makeup.

"It's weird that Skylenna and Dessin aren't here, huh?" Niles pulls me away from his chest to clean up the runny black smudges from my cheeks with his thumb.

I shake my head. "No. The Demechnef's have ruined their lives. They shouldn't have to support or say goodbye to a man who cost them everything."

Niles pulls his lips behind his teeth. He looks off into the distance at the departing soldiers, the lingering musicians.

"But I would have thought they'd be here to support you. Us."

"I'm not bothered by it."

"Chekiss did seem weird yesterday." He furrows his brow. "I asked how they were getting along in the house. He was quiet for a long time before answering."

"What did he say?"

"*She just needs time.*"

3. The Emerald Wife

Ruth

It's one of the worst nights since I've been here.

They tell me the fever is close to breaking. The medicine is working. Yet I'm in unimaginable pain, my legs scream so loud they wake me from a dead sleep, and I tremble so hard from the chills that I fear my heart will give out.

"It's almost over," Warrose says from across the room, watching me shiver with his knuckles turning white.

I can't even speak. My bones rattle. My brain swells and pulsates under my skull. My eyeballs weigh a thousand pounds.

"What can I do?" he asks in a low voice, pained and impatient. "I'll build a goddamned fire next to your bed if I have to."

I wish he would just leave. He doesn't need to see this. It's honorable to stay with me after all I've been through, but he doesn't need this burden—this obligation in his life.

"D-don't worry a-about it," I stammer.

I wonder if this is how Skylenna felt after going into the void and doing some real damage to our enemies. Freezing in a violent winter storm on the inside. Every inch of her body being solidified in blocks of ice. Why is my fever so high yet my body feels so cold?

"I know you don't want to be touched." Warrose is now hovering over my bed like the angel of death, brilliant in size, looming like the shade from a tree.

I can smell him from this distance. That smoky fire with lush spices and soap.

If I wasn't so horribly ill, I'd inhale deeper to capture that lovely scent.

"But just for tonight. I promise to be gentle with you," he says in a raw, husky voice.

Be gentle? "W-what?"

Warrose lifts my thick, heavy blankets off my trembling body, letting in a gust of icy air. And in nothing but a pair of soft pants, he climbs into bed next to me. Without a word, his bulging, tattooed arms are surrounding my frail figure. That bare chest is flush to my back. His breath seeps into my hair. And as if trying to protect me from the infection, to barricade my sick frame against outside forces that would try to hurt me, he cocoons his body around mine.

The instant comfort sends a rush of heat and relief down my spine, softening my muscles, sucking the deranged ache from my very soul.

We sigh in unison.

The feeling of being held when you're this sick is a remedy that cannot be overlooked. Yes, I've shouted from the rooftops for no one to touch me. To be left alone. To rot by myself.

But, my God, his arms are a cure.

I've never felt safer.

As he tightens around me—protectively, tenderly—our breaths fall into sync, and sleep, for the first time without nightmares, drapes over this cocoon.

"Thank fuck." Deep, morning voice.

Sunrise peeking through the curtains. The smell of cleaning

products. Coffee. A stale, old infirmary.

I try to blink the sleep away, but ultimately, it's the sensation of wet sheets that sends me in an adrenaline-rush panic. My eyes go wide.

"You sweat the fever out. Are you feeling a little better?" Warrose asks, still in bed next to me.

I sigh, relieved I didn't have another accident.

Sleepily, I pat myself down, examining for aches, pains, and chills. Nothing. I'm no longer shaking, no longer sore down to my eye sockets. I feel relatively better.

"I do," I respond quietly.

But then I attempt to stretch my legs. To roll my ankles. And the horror, the dread, the sinking pit in my stomach comes back as reality floods my senses once again.

Will this feeling ever go away?

"Water," I croak. But really, I want him out of my bed. Out of my room. I want to be alone when this ache in my soul takes over.

Warrose climbs out of bed. "Of course. I'll have someone change the sheets."

He seems so relieved, like we're halfway to the finish line. It breaks my heart. Doesn't he know? I wasn't hoping to survive that infection.

While he's away, I roll over to peer out through the grimy window. The towering Emerald Mountains in the distance. Rolling green hills. A rich sunrise blaring through the glass.

My stomach gurgles with hunger even though eating sounds rather frightening at the moment. I haven't been able to keep anything down because of the infection. My throat is raw from a consistent stream of stomach acid, and my abdominal muscles are so sore from convulsing, they throb from the slightest movement.

"You awake yet, sweet little rabbit?"

I flinch at Apple May's cold, greasy voice. Her coffee-scented breath brushes my ear and curdles inside my nostrils. As I turn slowly, I see her big towel-wrapped head hovering over my left side, perched on the side of the bed that Warrose slept on.

"Get. Out."

Apple May sneers before relaxing her face. "Hasn't your mother ever taught you manners?"

I close my eyes and grit my teeth. Agitation simmers in my gut because I can't do anything to protect myself. I'm not Skylenna, I can't send her to the void. I'm not Dessin. I'm not Warrose. Hell, even Niles could take this idiot.

With long, spindly fingers, the pretentious woman on my bed snatches my chin and forces me to look into her small gray eyes. As I focus on her irises, I note that the whites are yellow with small, irritated veins web on the inner corners.

"It's also polite to speak when you're spoken to, sweet little rabbit," she says with a glassy smile.

"I wasn't taught to show manners to those who dump vomit on my chest," I say through my teeth. That acidic smell finds its way back to me, burning my eyes on entrance.

The bitter Emerald Wife studies my face for a moment, her eyes trace my cheekbones, then the corners of my eyes. It's as if she's searching for wrinkles.

"I like the gentleman you're with," she comments like I haven't responded at all.

The mention of Warrose sends a flame of anger down my chest.

"He smiled at me when we walked past each other in the hallway. It was a smile of carnal attraction, I'm certain of it."

Oh, God. Give me a break.

I roll my eyes, but Apple May gives my chin an evil little shake to refocus my gaze back on her.

"Does he use you as a lady sex doll? I've heard of women being shipped to Demechnef soldiers, sedated and primed for them." This thought seems to excite her. "Does he have large genitalia?"

"What?"

This woman makes me miss the infection and isolation.

Her small eyes slide down to my sheets. "I bet your kitty cat is all torn up from his male needs. Should I take a look?"

My limbs shake in a sudden burst of fury.

"If you do, I won't be able to stop him from harming you," I threaten. Because, what else do I have? It's not like I can harm her myself. It's not like I have any power to hurt anyone at all.

"Or would he laugh with me? Are you embarrassed of the damage to your labia?" She purses her lips in thought. "You can't find my husband's penis with a microscope."

"What the fuck is your problem?" *Seriously. Did they check me into the asylum without my knowledge?*

"If you're going to take all of the attention away from me here, the least you can do is give me his in return."

Apple May reaches down my sheets and squeezes the tender, throbbing space where my leg ends. The healing wound. The sewn skin where my nerves are at their strongest. I release a banshee-like scream, bucking and arching toward the ceiling as a fiery wave of burning pain snakes up my thigh. The pain brings me back to the stage, waiting for a punishment I didn't know would be so drastic. So *permanent*. I'm there again, waiting, watching, hearing the cheers and silence of the audience.

"Tell him what I did, and I'll defecate into your next meal," she whispers in my ear.

Tears plunge from my eyes in a hot flood that races past my chin. The pain. The pain. The pain. It will never stop! It's going to last forever. It's unbearable! Someone help me!

"Help her!" Apple May shrieks by my side, weeping without tears as she examines me like a worried mother. "Please, someone help her!"

I'm unable to think clearly. The anguish fuses with every fiber in my brain. It sends me down a whirlpool of awful memories in the prison. Shivering on the cold, hard floor. Vomiting. Waking up behind bars. Watching my friends cry for me.

"What happened?" Warrose. It's Warrose.

"I heard her crying in here! Please, get some help. She's in so much pain!" Apple May puts on the show of her life, sniffling dryly, and wiping imaginary tears.

"Ruth? Can you tell me what hurts?" That patient, rough voice pierces through the vein of my agony.

All I can do is point to my left leg.

Two nurses rush into the room to administer pain medicine to me.

"What can I do to help?" Apple May asks him with a fragile hand on her chest.

Warrose doesn't seem to notice she's speaking to him because all he's doing is watching me wail with a clenched jaw as he's white knuckling the bed frame. So, the foul woman hops off my bed and hobbles over to him on her cane, placing a hand on his thick shoulder.

"Please, can I do something to help?" she asks again with a soft, eerie voice.

Warrose spares her a single glance, then returns his eyes back to me. "I was getting her breakfast before I heard the screaming."

"I can do that!" Apple May bubbles with eagerness.

I start shaking my head at him. *Please, no.* Do not let her go near my food.

He narrows his eyes at my sudden movement, then lifts his chin. "No. I'll get it myself once she's asleep."

The devious Emerald Wife juts out her lip and pouts. "Well, if you need anything. I mean, *anything* at all…I'm the room on the right."

4. This Very Special Room

Marilynn

Niles misses his family.

Ruth won't let us see her. Skylenna and Dessin are holed up in their cottage surrounded by the radiant red oaks with Chekiss and DaiSzek. He feels left out, forgotten, unloved.

It breaks my heart.

We've been staying in my house, the one Skylenna visited when she needed counseling after her interaction with Patient Thirteen in the asylum.

I look out the smudged window, watching Niles sit by the small pond in my backyard, throwing pieces of bread to a flock of ducks that isn't there.

I'd like to tell him why Skylenna, Dessin, and Chekiss aren't around him right now… But it isn't my place. When I heard that part of the prophecy as a little girl, I cried for three days. It felt like a special happy ending had been erased from the pages of their story.

There are many disadvantages to my situation. Knowing what I know. Having to watch it all play out without getting involved. It's a burden that sits like a rusted blade in my heart. It made me rebellious early on. It made me want to write my own fate. To ignore the stories and close my heart off to the golden boy who everyone loves.

But there is one advantage.

I might know Niles better than anyone in the world.

And therefore, I know how to make him feel better.

"Niles?" I poke my head out the window, being greeted by the breeze carrying the promise of cool autumn weather.

He lifts his head to acknowledge my voice but doesn't turn around. With a flick of his wrist, he tosses another handful of bread to the duck-less pond.

"I'm trying to move something, but it's just so heavy." I make an effort to appear worn out, as if I've been attempting this labor for quite a while.

Niles pops up, jogging through the scattered dandelions to throw open the back door.

"You're not supposed to lift anything!" he scolds with a mouthful of bread.

"Well, come on then."

He follows me through the vintage hallway, lined with copper walls and dispersed paintings. The bedroom on the right is cracked open, tickling my stomach nerves with butterflies as I try and imagine his reaction.

As I push the empty door open, Niles lets out a small gasp.

Rolled wallpaper sits in a heap on the fluffy gray carpet, greenery, plants, twinkling string lights to hang on the ceiling, a bronze bin of toys, and a bronze framed crib.

"Nursery?" he mutters, scanning the contents on the floor.

I strain my neck to look up at his speechless expression. Those round, innocent eyes. The gentle glow of his golden skin. And it takes everything within the parameters of my control not to start weeping at how much joy this brings me. I've thought often of how he would be in real life. I've committed myself to staying away, detaching, disconnecting immediately.

But look at him.

He's perfect.

I've never met a kinder soul.

A bigger heart.

"You want me to help set up the nursery?" he asks.

"I really would."

That pearly white grin spreads like an ocean's sunrise across his face. This very special smile makes me smile back, bigger than I have in my entire life. He meets my eyes with delirious glee before lifting me off my feet, pulling me flush to his body as he spins me through the air.

"Of course, I'll help!" He laughs, kissing the top of my forehead as he sets me back down. "Okay, so what's the theme? What're we going for? Obviously, it's a boy. But blue is so three years ago, right? Let's go big. Let's go magical!"

I snicker as he places frenzied pecks on my warm cheeks.

"I was thinking…Enchanted Kingdom theme?" I point to the wallpaper. "It's the backdrop of a castle and forest."

Niles gazes at the walls, closing one eye and tilting his head to the right.

"It's…PERFECT!"

"Really?"

I can't help but wonder how involved Aurick would have been during these precious moments of pregnancy. He would have been busy, available for the big moments, but I know he would have been very happy to be a father. The thought makes me sad. But I need this right now. I need Niles's enthusiasm. I need his fun energy and happy face.

I have always been a delicate but vital little figurine in this prophecy.

A puppet.

A piece to be moved.

I want this pregnancy to be for me. To be filled with happiness and not dread.

Niles bounces up and down on his heels. "He's basically a little prince! We have to get started right away. You hungry? Of course, you are. I'll make cookies and sandwiches."

As he jogs out of the nursery, I place my hands over my heart in silent gratitude. He's happy again. The golden boy who can light a room with his smile is beaming at something I did.

And with that smile, he'll help me build this very special room.

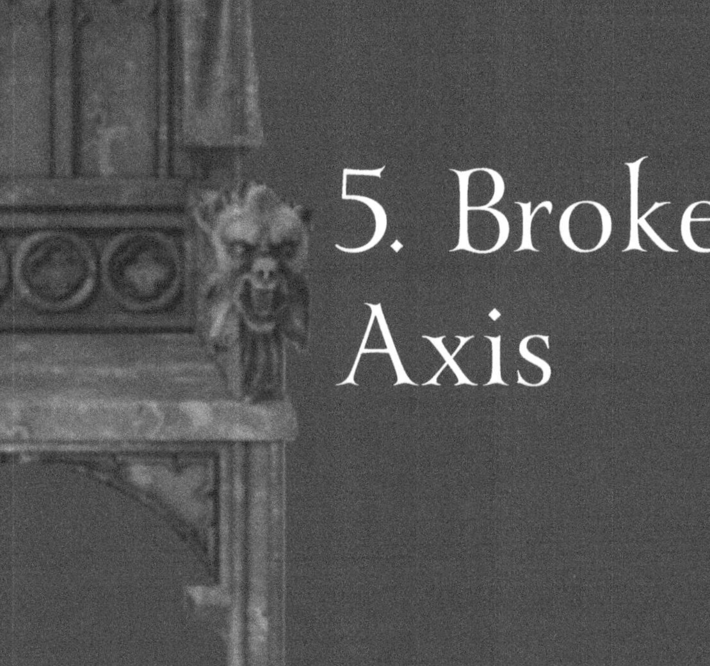

5. Broken Axis

Ruth

Niles and Marilynn tried to visit today.
I told the nurses to send them away.
I was tempted to say the same about Warrose.

"Wait right here," Nurse Aggie says, bustling out of the room excitedly. "We'll go get it!"

"Get what?"

I'm sore and unstable as they sit me upright on the edge of my bed. I look over at Warrose standing with his hands in his pockets in the corner of the room. It's strange seeing him with a shirt on, after so much time in the prison seeing his bare chest and back. He looks just as confused as I feel.

I hear the creaking before I see them drag it in.

Wooden legs with straps and pretty black shoes. My heart crinkles around the edges as if brushed by a flame. Nurse Aggie and Nurse Fionna walk in with huge, doll-like grins carrying the props as if they're made of gold. And I'm sinking in my seat, detaching from my body, dissociating entirely.

Warrose takes a cautious step forward.

"So, what do you think?" Nurse Fiona beams.

It's the new reality that is warping my spine and cutting off my air supply. It's the permanence of it all that sticks to the sides of my throat.

I will never walk again.

I will never run again.

I should have died in that prison.

At some point, Warrose has moved across the room to kneel at my side. His thick fingertips brush my wet cheekbones. Have I started crying? Have I really lost the ability to notice when tears run down my face?

"Are those tears of joy or sadness?" he asks.

An achy, unyielding pain hammers through my chest as the cry winds tighter into my bones. I'm flushed with resentment that is powerful enough to reject my sanity and send it flying far, far away.

"Ruth?"

The muscle cramps. The breaths of waterless air. The full bladder. The backside rash. The agonizing jolts of pain. The nightmares of being left behind. The axe. The fountain of blood. The moldy ceiling as Dessin performed surgery. The vomit spilling onto my cage floor. The sounds of Niles crying as I sleep. The baritone of Kaspias's laugh. The rotten scent of my blood and urine. The all-consuming, unrelenting depression.

A scream scorches my lungs, shredding my vocal chords as I throw my hands to the bed in defeat. The wails skid across the floor, ricocheting down the hallway. And Warrose doesn't flinch at my outburst.

I buckle down as I bawl without limitations, fighting the tremors and furor of emotions that want to break my body in half.

How can this happen? Why haven't I woken up from this nightmare?

I'll never walk again.

I'll never run again.

I should have died in that prison.

"Please leave," Warrose orders the nurses.

I shake my head back and forth, belligerent with anger and

heartbreak. Snot, tears, sweat, rashes, aches, sores.

"GET OUT!" I slam my hands down on the creaky mattress. "EVERYONE GET THE FUCK OUT!"

The nurses scurry out of the room, tripping over themselves as they both try to drag the wooden legs through the doorway.

Warrose places a hand on my back.

"You too!" I glare at him through swelling eyes. "Leave and don't come back!"

At this, he flinches.

"I'm not leaving you."

My fury is a meteor shower across the sky. A cloud of fire that burns through the atmosphere. It has no beginning or end.

"Don't you get it? I don't want you around! *I. Don't. Want. You!*"

Warrose tries not to let his face show how much my words have stabbed him in the heart. He grinds his jaw and doesn't break eye contact.

What does he see when he looks at me like this? I have snot running down my face. My eyes are sunken in. My olive skin is now the color of a corpse. My hair is matted and frizzy. And I am no longer pretty. I'm ugly. I'm useless. I'm sad. I'm broken.

"Leave! Leave! Leave! Don't ever come back!" I scream at him until I start coughing hysterically, choking and hiccuping on my crying fit. "GET OUT!"

At this point, even Warrose can see that his presence is doing more harm than good as I wear myself out to the point of hysteria and hostility. My body thrashes about like a wild animal, cornered and wounded.

"Please let me help you. God, don't make me leave." His voice is brittle. An image of dry, withering branches before being swept under a forest fire.

I wish I could stop this. There's that small voice in the back of my head begging me to spare him.

But alas, these words win the battle, forging their way to the tip of my tongue.

"You think I ever wanted you? Being in Kaspias's arms with his tongue down my throat was more exciting than being with you. Fucking leave!"

And I can see it.

That axe finds its way across the Midnight Sea and plunges into the center of Warrose's chest. His shoulders slump in resolution as he nods in understanding. But he has no words for me. Nothing to combat my vocal daggers as he exits my infirmary room and…

He doesn't come back.

The icy cold feeling of shame, disappointment, and self-hatred fills me to the brim. Why did I say things I can never take back? Why did I wound him so deeply after all he's done for me?

My kiss with Kaspias wasn't consensual. It was forced through Mind Phantoms. But I cherish every moment, every touch I had with Warrose in that prison.

I don't know why I want him to leave this infirmary forever.

And why I'm so devastated that he actually left. I all but shoved him out the door myself, so shouldn't I be relieved? Did I want him to fight for me? To insist that he would never leave my side? To prove that he still has feelings for me? Of course, he doesn't. But God, I want to believe so badly I'm still worth loving. Still worth fighting for.

Instead, I watched him disappear from that doorway like the last ray of sunshine exiting the coffin I'm buried alive in.

And I'm terrified he'll never come back.

6. Rotting Slowly

Ruth

Nurse Aggie tugs on my new catheter to ensure it's safely inserted inside me.

I stare blankly at the grimy window, watching the amber sunset lower over the blurry horizon. I wonder if I pray hard enough, maybe my soul will leave my body, maybe my spirit will fly away, chasing the sun as it sleeps below the earth.

"That feel okay?"

I don't answer.

I made my protests already. No one listened.

But I suppose that's what I get for wetting the bed again during my nightmares.

"Darling, you must eat first thing in the morning, yes? Force-feedings are terribly unpleasant."

Force-feedings.

Just let me fucking die!

Why can't anyone see how horrible my quality of life is? Why can't anyone understand how I'll never be greeted by the sweet kiss of happiness again? I no longer allow visitors. I no longer accept food past my lips. I hardly take a sip of water.

My life is an endless pit of misery, and I want out!

And even though I miss Warrose hanging around, sleeping on a cot by my bed, reading me books and singing songs to help me fall asleep, I'm glad he's gone.

He doesn't need to feel obligated to care for me.

He deserves a beautiful woman who can care for him.

Though, I still yearn for him deeply, profoundly, unwarrantedly. It's an ache between my breasts, sulking past my strongest walls.

"Blink if you can hear me," Nurse Aggie says cautiously.

My eyelashes flutter. They've been asking me this often as of late. Perhaps worried I'm falling into a catatonic oblivion that will end in my imminent death. I don't speak anymore. Not really. My words feel meaningless, empty, and without any weight. Once they leave my lips, they float in the wind, disintegrating like an effervescent tablet in water.

"Good," she coos. "How long has it been since that big, beautiful man has stopped by? I know you put a restriction on all visitors, but did you have to deprive us nurses of such eye candy?"

She's trying to make me laugh. It's a sad attempt.

"It's been at least a week and a half," she comments while tucking me under my blankets.

A week and a half. Has it really been that long?

Clearly no longer understanding my own feelings, the urge to cry pressurizes in my throat. I hold my breath until it becomes a toxic substance in my lungs, praying for her to leave so I can fall apart in silence.

I miss my entire family. I miss running in the forest with DaiSzek. I miss Skylenna's airy laugh and Niles's stupid jokes. I miss Dessin's funny way of showing he cares about me. I miss Warrose with my whole heart.

But I don't miss any of them enough to sentence them to watch me rot slowly.

Within a lapse of time I can't count or keep track of, my mind wanders into a tortuous nightmare. One with flashes of yellow and red lights, of a ringmaster stomping his cane, of inmates being beaten and whipped.

I never really escaped that prison.

The sharp stomach pains drag me by my phantom ankles out of the darkness.

I grip my core as I roll to my side, wincing, gasping, waiting for the cramping to pass. First signs of starvation, isn't it? We all had a taste for it in the prison. But now I'm growing impatient. When will my organs shut down? When will I get to leave this body?

"You're threatened by me." Apple May's toweled silhouette appears in the light of the moon from my window. "That's why you sent him away."

I don't bother responding. She can kick and throw a tantrum all she wants. She can do whatever she wants to me. I don't care anymore.

"You didn't want to have to hear me sucking and slurping on his cock through these thin walls, did you?" She slips into my bed quietly, moving with the grace of a kitten. "He would have begged for the warm respite of my mouth. I would have swallowed every drop of that beautiful man's semen."

I squeeze my eyes shut against those horrible fucking images.

"And that threatens you more than anything, doesn't it? Your torn up little cunt would have been a distant memory."

The scent of cigarettes and scotch are pungent on her tonight.

Moments pass in the darkness of her staring at me creepily.

"You look like you're about to die, sweet little rabbit. Did you know that?" she asks with fake concern.

I hope so.

"If that's the case, then I suppose I can tell you my real problem with you. Because in fact, it isn't really with you at all. It's with the woman you're supposedly friends with."

I open my eyes again to stare into that bleak, hateful gaze.

"The blonde woman who burned the asylum to the ground. My daughter worked there, you know." Apple May strokes my cheek as if she has an ounce of a maternal side to her. "Her name was Meridei."

Jesus. She's fucking Meridei's mother?! That is the greatest explanation I could have received for her foul behavior.

"And once I get out of here, I'm going to burn that cute little cottage blondie built in the Red Oaks to the ground."

"How—"

She scoffs. "I'm an Emerald Wife. I have people working for me, waiting for the blond arsonist to get back into town. They reported back to me the location where she currently resides. I'm just biding my time before I make her pay for killing my daughter in that fire."

I process what she's saying as all my other ailments leave me in peace for a few long seconds, making room for a white, flaming streak of rage. And my body radiates heat and an icy chill with the world going silent around me.

I may not be able to care for my own wellbeing right now, but caring for my family is effortless. I would die to protect my friends.

Apple May grins wide, revealing a glassy set of artificial teeth.

"Not that Skylenna needs my help, but still…" I trail off, imagining the way she would toy with this insane woman's mind. DaiSzek catching Apple May with a match before she got close to their home. And Dessin, well, knowing him—he may already know of this evil plan to hurt the woman he loves.

I don't care. All that matters now is that she has threatened to burn their home to the ground. She threatened my best friend in the whole world.

In a swift jabbing motion, I poke my two long thumbnails into Apple May's eyeballs. The nails are so sharp and pointed, there is a gushing sound as I rip into her cornea and *dig* in.

Through her kicking and howling, I hold on tight. Bearing down against the bruises and scratches she's laying on thick to my body. I'm made of stone. Unfeeling. Uncaring.

And as I pull my bloody thumbs from her lids, I lean into her flailing, crying head and whisper, "Enjoy trying to get past a RottWeilen completely *blind*."

I let her fall to white tile floor in heaping gasps. My head falls back on my pillow in peace, ignoring the pounding heart in my chest and throat.

After several seconds, I wonder why no one has raced into my room to help the cruel Emerald Wife. Meridei's goddamned *mommy*.

Suddenly, the gas lamps slowly grow bright in the hallway. One flicker at a time. A clattering of metal hits the floor. A door swinging off its hinges. Yelps. Feminine bickering.

I lift my head an inch from my pillow, narrowing my lids to get a better look out of the small window on my door.

"You can't be in here!" a nurse barks.

White uniforms flash across that glass, barely visible with the dim gas lamp lighting.

"Out! Out!"

"We'll have you arrested!"

I can only picture Dessin making a break in like this. It's his style. To save me? To make sure I eat again? Has my friend come to finally see me?

My infirmary door opens to the chaos in the hallway, revealing shoulders so broad and wide they nearly touch the edges of the doorframe. Warrose is an immovable oak tree as the nurses swat and shove his back from behind, though he doesn't flinch or seem to notice their attempts in the slightest. And with his massive frame blocking the light from the hall, I can't see his facial expression. Only the rapid movement of his warrior's chest.

"I'm taking her home," he announces gruffly, in the special morning voice that sounds like crackling wood or gravel under tires. "If you think your security can stop me, give it your best fucking shot."

I'm instantly wide awake at this intrusion. Normally, I may yell at him to leave. Remind him of all the horrid things I've said to him before. But I'm so weak, so sad, so alone. My heart tears in three places, swelling and splitting as he takes two long strides to my bedside.

"Home?" I croak.

Warrose lowers himself to one knee, thoughtfully examining my face, shoulders, arms, and hands. His dark brows pull together, and his eyes start to gloss over as if just looking at my withering appearance might make him cry.

"Yes, baby girl. I'm taking you home."

A whimper escapes my throat as tears pulse over my dry eyes. I nod, holding my quivering arms out to him in a silent plea to do it now. Take me away.

Warrose clears his throat as he melts a little at my attempt to latch on to him. With one careful motion, he wraps his giant arms under my thighs and around the middle of my back. And I'm plucked from the metal-framed bed, effortlessly pulled to the warmth of his chest.

He pauses to stare down at the writhing, nasty, cruel woman on the floor, clutching her bloody eye sockets. Those dark hazel eyes flick back to my thumbs, then up at me. I simply sigh.

"Move," he barks at the nurses gathering in the doorway.

They squeal and flee as he strides into the hallway, unconcerned with the many employees gawking and whispering as he carries me securely off the premises.

I nuzzle against his black shirt, clutching his collar with Apple May's blood transferring from my skin to his fabric. I breathe him in and let my tears soak through the cotton. I can feel the weight of his gaze peering down at me, but I keep my eyes shut.

"I told you not to come back," I choke out.

His breath pauses in its steady rhythm. "I remember."

"I said horrible things." My mind skips back to that final moment I wounded him so deeply. How can we ever come back from that? How could he want to be around me still?

"Yes."

"Then why did you come back?" I press.

What answers am I looking for? I peer up at him through foggy, sore eyes. And I'm terrified that his answer will only make me feel more like a burden.

"Don't say it's because you think I need you. Plea"

"Because *I* need *you*, Ruth. Every night I've spent away from your bedside has been sad and lonely. I don't even remember a time before you. What was my life like before I heard your voice? And the thought of my life happening *after* you is what sent me barreling through those infirmary doors."

I stop breathing and go stiff in his arms. My eyes are sticky and slow as I blink up at his face, a masculine silhouette in the shimmering moonlight. My insides turn to a warm putty.

And we're quiet for a long, long time as he walks down a cobblestone street, passing streetlamps, boutiques, and the occasional fainting couch. All I can think about during these wordless moments is the fear of letting my heart open too much. I want so badly to accept those pretty words and hold him tight, kiss his chest, say sweet words back.

But what happens when he tires of this new version of me?

What happens when he one day decides to leave?

I can't take that new pain. My body and mind are already in enough turmoil.

"Talk to me, Ruth. What happened to that woman? What did she do to you?"

My soul shrinks at the thought of breathing life into any of the words that have just crossed my mind.

With more tears shining in my eyes, I say "I'm so tired, War."

"I know, little rebel. I know."

7. The Old Ways

Marilynn

Glass shattering is an unmistakable noise.

Even in a dead sleep, I wake in delirium, knowing the clattering sound as soon as it reaches my ears.

My bare feet patter along the old wood floors as I turn the corner of the hallway, spotting Niles already ahead of me, shirtless and hair uncombed. He comes to a halting stop in the living room, whipping his arm out to stop me from taking another step forward.

"What is it?" I ask, blinking rapidly to clear my vision of the lingering sleep.

Niles pulls his gaze from the floor to meet my eyes with a firm wrinkle between his brows. I poke my head around him to see the brick in the middle of the floor, surrounded by a field of broken glass. The window by the front door is now an open channel for the morning breeze. The sheer curtains ripple around the jagged frame lined with shards.

Niles places a hand on my shoulder. "Wait here, please."

"Like hell," I mutter, following behind him.

"I'm not letting you go out there until I know it's safe." Serious. That furrowed brow. Such a rare sight.

After a moment, he returns with a sigh.

I'm careful to step around the pile of glittering carnage, feeling a pit forming in my stomach at the message someone is trying to send us.

Niles shuffles behind me, throwing on his slippers, then scrambling to lift me off my feet.

"Niles!" I gasp, clutching my hands to the back of his neck for support.

"What?" His slippers crunch through the glass as he walks us to the broken window. "I'm protecting your feet."

I bite my lip against the slow creeping smile.

Through the gaping window, we peek out at the early morning light blanketing the driveway. Not a soul in sight. But something still feels wrong, like we aren't getting the full picture.

As we step outside to further investigate the damage, Niles sets me down, and I walk out to the open, uncut lawn.

"I'd rather you not look." Niles calls out to me. "I'll clean it up."

Clean what?

Oh.

I'm facing the house now. The white panels now defaced with red paint. The words like melting iron dumped over my head. I knew this would come, but I suppose I didn't expect it to feel like a fist swinging into my gut.

WOMEN CAN'T RULE.

WOMEN CAN'T RULE.

WOMEN CAN'T RULE.

Red mocking words. Giant letters. A statement that was meant to wound and bruise and infect. *Women can't rule.*

"Who would write this?" Niles continues to stare.

I sigh. "Unfortunately, a great many people."

After announcing Aurick's death to the government, I announced my claim on his title. I am a Blackforth. And since this organization used to be called *Demechforth*, due to our two lineages running the ship together, it's only fitting and my birthright.

"You're not surprised by this." He's staring at me now, turned around and watching my stoic expression cautiously.

I shake my head.

"Why not?"

"Because after I announced my claim on Aurick's title and position, I knew what I was walking into. Women here are meant to look pretty and follow strict rules. I'm a woman, and I'm demanding these men follow *my* rules. It contradicts the careful layout of their entire society. Of how they were raised."

Niles snags a lock of my shimmering red hair, studies it thoughtfully. "Are you in danger?"

"Most likely."

"Then we need to tell Dessin and Skylenna."

"No. I can handle this myself. They won't touch me as long as I'm carrying a male heir that will carry on both lineages."

"But they will try to scare you." He points over his shoulder at the red paint.

"Yes."

"How often?"

"As many chances as they get until I'm too afraid to make any real decisions on my own without the final say from male representatives," I answer darkly.

Niles tucks that strand of hair behind my ear. "Then every chance we get, we're going to have fun, right?"

"Are we?"

"Yes, Marilynn." His thumb caresses my cheekbone sweetly, raising goosebumps across my freckled shoulders. "We'll erase every bad moment with a good one."

I fight the galloping of my heart like I'm trying to steady a wild horse.

"What kind of good ones?" My words come out breathy and weak.

"Fun, happy, loving." Niles leans down to brush his lips over my cheek, over the tingling spot he's been caressing.

I close my eyes in a drunken haze. "Yes."

"I promise not to let any of the bad creep in," he whispers, breath stroking my ear and making my toes curl against the dewy blades of grass. His hand finds my growing belly and rubs it in circles.

"Okay."

And he places another kiss on the corner of my mouth. Not close enough to have any real contact with my lips, but enough to make a flood of heat hit my lower belly.

"Do you want to make breakfast with me?" he asks.

I can only nod. My eyes flutter open. The morning sun burns my retinas, but through my lashes, Niles is glowing. That halo of soft hair. Those gorgeous eyes and white smile.

He's the golden boy of the story.

The one I've been running from.

And despite my best efforts, he *is* my sun.

8. Resuscitation

Ruth

Fifty different smells wake me up.

I stare at the ceiling of a sheer canopy overhead. This room is familiar. It's a brief mist of déjà vu that trickles across my thoughts. The walls are maroon with golden designs of angels and tree branches. A walnut vanity with jars of creams and oils. A fireplace crackling across the room.

For the first time in…I'm not sure how long, I'm deeply comfortable. It's a feather bed with thick, warm blankets and silk sheets. I'm not sure where Warrose brought me, but I'm so grateful to be out of that stiff hospital bed. It made my lower back scream with a lingering ache that seemed to vibrate through my bones. The squeaking springs woke me every time I turned on my side.

Heavy footsteps creak outside the bedroom door followed by a brief knock.

"Ruth?" That gravelly voice makes my sleeping heart pick up its pace.

"I'm up."

The door opens, and Warrose steps inside. The gust of air that wafts through the open door carries the aroma of a bakery. Warm butter and sugar.

"May I carry you downstairs?" he asks.

I give myself a quick pat down under the heavy white comforter to check if I'm clothed. It's a nightgown. I nod once. But that sick feeling forms a puddle in my gut. *Carry me. Care for me. Spend all your time with me.*

"Where are we?" I ask, pushing those dark thoughts down.

"Aurick's estate. Haven't you been here before?" Warrose pulls my covers off me, hooking his arms around my body to lift me off the bed. His dark gray shirt has an open chest, with sleeves that roll up to his elbows. I lean my face against his shoulder as he secures me to him. The natural heat seeping off his chest smells like him and soap. Clean and musky.

Wait, is this…?

"This is Skylenna's old room," I say with a small gasp.

"Marilynn said we could stay here."

A twist of shame and sorrow warp my spine. I've pushed everyone away. But then again, why hasn't Skylenna tried to visit me?

Warrose walks me down the stairs and into the dining room. The smell of a bakery and buffet are potent down here, making my stomach gurgle loudly.

"Good. I was worried you weren't going to be hungry." Warrose laughs.

The long rectangular table is set with several different options. A basket of muffins, a plate of pancakes, bowls of fruit, bacon, eggs, sausage, and coffee. My mouth parts, and I stare up at Warrose in surprise.

"Did you do all of this?"

He nods.

"How long did it take you?" I huff, turning back to the steaming table.

"Hours."

Hours. For me?

"I'll eat most of it. But I wanted you to have options," he clarifies.

Heat flushes and stains my cheeks.

Hours.

There's too much food. I'm going to disappoint him if I don't eat as much as he thinks I should. It's going to go to waste. All of his time preparing this will go to waste.

Panic grips my throat with its cold, leathery hand.

"Will you be upset with me if I don't eat much?" I ask as he sits me down in a red velvet chair. My thighs throb from the pressure, but I'm just happy to not be lying in a bed all day.

Warrose shakes his head. "No. And it was wrong of me to ever give you a hard time with that. Not to mention, I read your file at the infirmary. You haven't been eating at all. I think it's safer if you only have a small portion of food to reintroduce your stomach to food."

He drops into the seat to my left, loading our plates with a little of everything. My mouth waters at the blueberry muffins and the pancakes. The thick syrup glowing a rich amber in the morning light.

I pick at a strawberry, then pieces of the muffin. It's all so good. But after three bites of a buttered pancake drenched in syrup, I push my plate away. That's going to show up as cellulite on my lower belly. A deep regret fills my lungs at the thought.

Warrose lays a heavy hand on top of mine.

"If that's as much as you want to eat today, that's okay. But just know, even though we're back in the Chandelier City, the lady-doll regimen is as good as gone now that Marilynn is working on taking over." He strokes a thumb over my knuckles.

I stay perfectly still under the warmth radiating from his calloused palm. He's watching me with those shining hazel eyes that seem to unravel bits of my soul. My heart ripples like raindrops falling into a pond.

"I don't just eat this way out of fear," I explain, licking my sticky lips. "I've been told since birth that this is what it takes to look beautiful."

Warrose winces, yet it's hardly noticeable, and he recovers quickly. His rough hand squeezes mine a little harder.

"I understand. But if it's any consolation, I'd think you were beautiful at any size, any shape, any form. All of your angles are beautiful."

The backs of my eyes start to sting, so I look down.

I take a shallow breath, peering at him in a new light. "Why are you doing all of this for me? Why stick around after everything I've said to you? After seeing how damaged I've become?"

He thinks on this for a long moment, thrumming his fingers over my wrist.

"I thought you were going to die in that community shower, little rebel. And then when you didn't, I was sure you weren't going to survive the night." His voice cracks and his eyes become glossy. "I prayed all fucking night while you slept in my arms. I prayed I'd get one more day with you. How wonderful does a woman have to be to get firmly rejected by her, and I still come crawling back just to be around her again?"

At this, I open my hand to him and let his fingers entwine with my own. I feel so small next to him, yet so important. So valuable.

"I'll try to eat more tomorrow."

Ruth

Weeks seem to pass by of me progressing, getting out of bed, eating a few more bites than before. But eventually, I regress just as fast. I stay in bed, lying alone in a cationic state. I reject food, convincing myself that the skin under my arms is fat. All from eating Warrose's food.

Depression. Sleep. Migraines. Fits of crying at night. Eating when I feel good. Regret for eating too much. It's a vicious cycle that exhausts both of us.

It's agony to flip through the emotions of shame from my eating habits, guilt for being a burden, and physical pain of my recovery. The constant self-deprecating thoughts come so close to taking me down.

Eventually, we arrive at somewhat of a stable routine.

Warrose carries me downstairs for breakfast, I eat a little more, and he takes me out to the garden to read. Some nights, he draws me a bath and takes my instructions on what herbs and concoctions to throw in there. Other nights, he sings to me until I fall asleep.

This afternoon, I felt good enough to tell him that I'd like to see my family again.

Only Niles and Marilynn join us.

I'm sitting on the edge of the fountain as I feel a pair of eyes on my back, watching me with a heaviness that trickles through the air. I tilt my head to the side just enough to see the gold hue of his hair like morning dew collecting over a sunflower.

"Ruthie?" His voice deflates on arrival.

"Hi, Niles."

With four giant strides, he closes the gap between us in this garden, slipping his arms around my waist and falling to his knees.

"I missed you," he chokes out into my lap. "God dammit I missed you so much."

My hands work their way into his soft hair, caressing him delicately as he breathes heavily against my dress.

"I'm sorry. I just needed time," I mutter. *It's been so hard. It's still so hard.*

Marilynn and Warrose stand off to the side watching us, giving us space, and talking among themselves.

"I know. It's just been hard. We spent so much time in that prison together, and just like that"he snaps his fingers together without looking up from my lap "I'm cut off from both you and Skylenna."

A jolt passes through my stomach. "You haven't seen Skylenna either?"

He shakes his head, face still buried in my lap.

"Niles." I tap the back of his neck for him to look at me. "It's not like her not to visit me…or at least *try* to visit me after everything. Where is she?"

His eyes shudder with a terrible thought. He opens his mouth to take a guess.

"She can explain herself."

A raspy voice cuts through the garden. All of our heads turn to Chekiss standing under the ivy archway near the back door. He looks so much older, so tired and sad.

"Chekiss!" Niles pops up from my lap, jogging over to give him a big hug.

Chekiss grunts at the impact of Niles's enthusiasm, chuckling softly as he pats the back of that golden head.

"Chekiss," I mutter thickly.

The man with crow's feet around his eyes, freckled cheeks, and a warm smile looks down at me fondly. "Hello, child."

I'm going to cry. My throat aches from the terrible lump forming. I reach out my arms to him, and he steps forward to embrace me without another word.

"I'm here when you're ready to talk about it," he whispers softly.

I nod against his shoulder, breathing through the urge to sob against his shirt. It's that gentle tone he uses, that hug resembling a grandfather. He truly is a grandfather to us all.

"Has something happened?" I ask.

Chekiss pulls away from our embrace. Those aged, algae-green eyes narrow, look away, then come back to the rest of us like he's bearing the weight of the world.

And yet, Marilynn seems to mirror his expression perfectly.

"You all must come with me now. It's time we reunite in the Red Oaks."

9. Weight of The World

Marilynn

I used to scream at my mother during this part of the story. I'd yell until my face turned purple. *Please, make him wake up! Make him wake up!*

These characters I grew attached to didn't deserve such a horrendous fate. They had the purest love, the strongest souls. How is there any justice in the world if this is the ending they receive?

And Niles has no idea what he's walking in on.

My legs shake as I step into Skylenna's beautiful cottage wrapped around the biggest Red Oak tree in these crimson woods. There are candles lit, and the house looks so clean, untouched, like a rustic museum that remains in pristine condition. Her shiny oak floors have been swept and mopped, the shelves with photographs of Skylenna and Kane as children have been dusted, and the air smells of warm vanilla sugar and cedar.

They've built a wonderful home.

If only this weren't their fate.

If only they could have enjoyed it.

"Chekiss, I'm worried. This doesn't feel right," Niles comments as he shuts the door.

Warrose adjusts Ruth in his arms. She straightens her back to look down the hall, searching for her best friend who hasn't come to visit her either.

My stomach bubbles with something sour and thick.

"Follow me," Chekiss says quietly, taking the lead down the hallway.

We come to a stop at the master bedroom. He knocks twice and pauses. Skylenna's faint voice responds through the muffled wood.

And we walk inside.

"What's going on?" Warrose asks with a higher octave of alarm lining his throat.

Dessin sleeps in the center of the bed, and Skylenna sits on the edge grasping his limp hand. His chest moves up and down, his face a blanket of peace. My throat tightens at the sight of it all.

Skylenna's shiny emerald eyes flash up to Warrose, and her brow knits like she's about to lose it at the sight of him, of all of us.

"I'm sorry I've been away," her voice breaks into a husk of a whisper. "But something's happened."

Niles goes still at my side.

"Get his ass out of bed, and then you can tell me," Warrose counters with a cold expression tightening his face.

And those emerald eyes line with more tears. She says nothing.

Warrose holds her stare for a moment too long, challenging her, fighting a truth he doesn't even know yet.

"Wake him up," he demands.

Niles's mouth parts as he watches his friends in silence.

Skylenna doesn't move.

"Dessin," Warrose calls out. "Dessin!"

"He's not going to wake up," she finally says.

"Dessin!"

Skylenna is on her feet, swift and graceful like a quiet cat. She touches his arm that is tightening around Ruth's body.

"Warrose, he'she's not going to wake up."

My lungs ache as Niles wavers in his stance.

"What happened?" Ruth asks.

Skylenna adjusts her footing, facing all of us. "They did something to him in those experiments. Kaspias injected him with a failsafe. A new chemical that would…place him in a coma the next time we became intimate."

"What?" Niles bursts.

"I've tried everything to wake him up."

I know the answer to my own question. Of course, I do. But I can't help but ask. I can't help but fight to have hope that I'm wrong. *Please, God, let me be wrong.*

"Can you find him and bring him back in the void?"

The saddest tears spill over her long, wispy bottom lashes.

"I've looked," she whispers wetly. "I've looked…*everywhere.*"

Skylenna's entire body starts to shake violently. Niles moves first, rushing to hold her up by her elbows.

"I can't find him. I can't find *any* of them!" *Any of his alters.*

A cloud of despair infects the room with its promise of permanent pain. And we all fall apart with her, gushing tears as she howls in agony.

"The inner world is gone! Ambrose Oasis is empty!"

It's all real. This part was real.

And Patient Thirteen would be so close to his soul mate, yet so very far away.

10. Goodbye to The Sun

Ruth

"Our love was supposed to conquer anything. We haven't had enough time. I haven't loved him long enough."

Warrose shifts across the bedroom in a slow, daunting walk. His eyes are fixated on Dessin's sleeping body. And within the parameters of his strong arms, I can feel him tremble.

Slowly, he lowers himself to sit next to Dessin's right side. There's a stillness before he pulls in a sharp breath. Dessin does not look peaceful. He does not look like he's sleeping.

He looks *gone*.

And Warrose doesn't say a word. He stares at his best friend with a clenched jaw and watering eyes. Gently, his left hand steadies me on his lap as he reaches to place his hand on top of Dessin's.

I squeeze my eyes shut against the tears.

And we sit here for several seconds before I can't take it anymore. My arms slide around his neck, and I pull him to my chest for a hug.

I'm so sorry.

Warrose's muscles contract, going rigid under my embrace. It's a brief moment of surprise, a pausing heartbeat. Then with his right hand, he circles my waist, tugging me flush against his core. His wide shoulders shudder as my breath grazes his neck, my tears splashing against his skin.

I'm so sorry, War-Man.

"There has to be something we can do," Warrose mutters in a husky voice.

"Well…" The bed shifts as Skylenna stands. "This wasn't the only news I have for all of you."

Warrose sighs against my collarbone before he loosens his grip around me, turning to face Skylenna. She walks around to the headboard, gazing down at her lost soul mate with so much despair it falls from her shoulders in waves.

"I'm pregnant." Her feathery voice breaks again, and she doesn't look away from Dessin's sleeping face. "I'm having his baby."

No sound.

No breath.

No heartbeats.

Our souls go utterly silent.

Pregnant.

Dessin.

Coma.

"I'm having his baby all by myself." Tears. So many tears. She strokes a finger across Dessin's cheekbone. More tears.

Pregnant.

"Oh my god," I gasp.

"You're…" Niles stumbles back. "You're what?"

"Are you certain?" Warrose asks. And *now*…now it sounds like he might fall to pieces. That rugged, edged voice wavers, bruised with heartbreak, making the cool air in this room unbreathable.

"Yes." She nods, wiping her face. "I can't even be mad. It's like he made sure to leave me with someone who will love me, so I won't be alone. It's like his soul knew what was coming."

Warrose chokes and turns away, looking back at his best friend with despair splotching his neck and cheeks. That one got him. That one statement tightened the noose around his neck, and he's struggling to breathe evenly. Those glowing hazel eyes water profusely.

"I brought every memory back to him before it happened. He finally looked at me again. I mean *really* looked at me." Skylenna wraps her arms around her core and squeezes like she's trying to relieve the pain. "I thought this was all finally over. The tragedy. The suffering. I thought…"

Helplessness ricochets over my limbs.

"You thought what?" I ask.

She draws her eyes away from his face to look at me. "I thought we finally found our happy ending. But we never really escaped that prison, did we?"

We didn't. I'm still trapped there in every nightmare. I'm still confronted by the axe. We are all still barred by the chains that were kept around our necks. Still confined in those terrible cages.

"You won't raise your baby alone, Skylenna. They're being born into an entire family." Warrose squeezes Dessin's hand. "We're going to love them enough for Dessin and Kane."

Skylenna looks down at Warrose with a devastating blend of gratitude and heartbreak. With a wet sob, she slowly collapses on Dessin's body, hugging his limp core to her as she cries, letting herself have this moment to splinter and crack down the middle.

And our family does the only thing we know how to do in this moment.

We gather around her to hold each other close.

To hug until the crying fit ends.

To hug because that's all we have left to give.

11. Midnight Snack

Marilynn

We stay with Ruth and Warrose tonight in Aurick's mansion. It isn't easy for me, walking these halls again. It's as if I'm stepping into a bubble of frozen time. Everything is where I left it before I disappeared. He never took down my decorations, never moved a single piece of art.

It's like Aurick Demechnef was waiting for me to come back to him.

The thought pinches my heart until there's a lack of blood circulation.

I turn in my bed to watch the full moon grow bright and abnormally large outside my bedroom window. The hunger pains gurgle around in my belly, fusing my gut with intense cravings that leave my mouth watering at the thought of pastries, cheeses, and lemon cookies.

"Can I come in?" Niles's sleepy voice slips through the crack in my door.

My heart picks up, charges my veins with adrenaline.

We always stay in our separate rooms at night.

He's so respectful. Too respectful.

"Yes," I whisper, rolling over to face him stepping over the threshold and closing the door behind him.

"Just let me know if you need more," he says quietly.

"Of what?"

Niles sets down a heavy wooden board stacked with lemon cookies, slices of aged cheese, and pickles. Everything I'm craving desperately.

"I brought milk too."

My heart gallops before it fumbles forward. "You did?"

"You don't think I hear you sneak into the kitchen every night to appease your cravings?"

I furrow my brow.

Niles laughs.

"Do you…" I prop myself up to sit under my thick feather comforter. "Do you want to eat with me?"

His lips part then close, then part again.

"You don't have to if you'd rather go back to"

"Yes!" he bursts. Niles wastes no time as he takes a seat at the foot of my bed, slipping a chocolate croissant off the tray.

I watch as his fingers pull apart the flaky bread. They're long, tan, and…attractive. I've never found hands attractive before. But Niles is perfect in all areas.

After a moment, his hands go still, no longer fidgeting with his croissant. I snap out of the brief trance, shooting my eyes up to his careful, watchful gaze.

"See something you like?" His sleepy voice rings through my ears.

"Yes." My voice cracks pathetically before I clear it. "The croissant looks good."

Niles glances down at his hands, then back to me slowly. He tears off a hunk of bread and brings it to my lips. His fingers are careful not to touch my mouth as he offers it up for me to take. But something bold and tingly races up my spine, blindly affecting my frontal lobe. I keep my eyes locked with his as I pull that piece of croissant into my mouth with my teeth. There's only a second to pause before I close my lips around the tip of his finger, tasting his skin and closing my eyes.

I hear a sharp inhale as I release him.

And as I let my eyes flutter open, I see him watching me with a lack of patience. A contained moment of frustration. But his expression returns to its natural state of cool acceptance.

"Good?" he asks without removing his eyes from my lips.

I nod. "Very."

After a long moment, he sets down his food, and leans in. And even though I'm itching to touch him, to be close to him, to taste his mouth again…

I pull away.

The action makes him pause, assessing my body language carefully. Trying to understand where he went wrong.

"You give me so many mixed signals, Marilynn."

Shame rushes through my core like a stormy currant. Why am I like this? Why can't I just let it happen? It's Niles. *Niles.* He doesn't deserve to have his heart tugged around like this.

"I know. I'm sorry."

Niles examines the inner workings of my blue eyes like he's digging deep gaping holes for answers. "Are you like this because…"

"Because what?"

He exhales slowly. "Because of what you know about the future?"

The weight of those words. The terrifying meaning hangs in the air like a sword over my head. The future. I know far too much. I know things that would make him hate me for not speaking out. I've battled this knowledge since I was a little girl.

It's not fair. It's not fair. It's not fair.

"Yes," I murmur thickly.

"I see." He nods with understanding, giving me a special smile that only Niles can give. "Well, what if I told you to put all of that into a locked box in the back of your head. I'll never pry for information. I'll never try to unlock that box. Will you let me in then?"

That wall I've spent years and years building in the gray, murky depths of my mind threatens to fall, then rise again. Strong. Secure. Unrelenting.

But those kind, gentle, sparkling eyes melt my greatest security defenses.

And tears well against my lids. My cheeks burn and throb as I hold in a cry that has been trapped in my chest since the age of five.

Niles Offborth, can't you see how I've longed to sit this close to you?

"I'll be your safe place away from all that you know but can't say. Okay?"

My hands tremble, mimicking the quaking feeling within my heart. And I begin to nod slowly, watching as a single tear swells over my bottom lashes, dribbling down my hot cheeks, falling into the palm of his golden hand.

And with that tear-streaked hand, he places his palm on the side of my face. "I feel like I've been waiting a lifetime for you to make the first move, sweetie. My lips are yours if you'll have them."

"I'll have them," I say in a rushed exhale. "Of course, I'll have them."

Throwing the board of food from the bed, I lunge in his arms, clinging to his cotton nightshirt as I crash my lips into his. And oh, how he tastes of sunny days and the sweetest plates of desserts. His mouth moves with such precision, such careful planning. Like he's thought about the way he'd kiss me for years and years. A delicate method to the rhythm of his tongue slipping past my lips, caressing the inside of my mouth.

His hands find the backs of my thighs, and so easily they pull me into his lap, gliding over my backside to fondle my curves with a patient, intimate touch. I wrap my legs around his backside, securing him closer to me.

Everything about the way he loves is so pure, so intentional, so lovely. Niles Offborth has never been a master at combat, a sadist monster to outsmart an enemy. He's been a loyal friend. A much needed moment of comedic timing. Niles Offborth has been a glimmering light in the face of imminent darkness.

We've known all of this.

But tonight, I see his greatest strength.

He's a passionate, profound lover.

He's turned traumatic experiences into a craft with so much beauty I could cry right here in his arms.

Overcome with a building need, I arch my back and thrust my hot center against his lap. I roll my hips over his long erection, and he reacts with a small sigh against my tongue.

"I want you tonight," I breathe.

Niles continues to kiss me, feeling his way around the underside of my ass, the softness of my inner thighs. It makes me clench around air, soaking my panties.

And it's as if he can sense the immediate reaction his wandering hands have caused. With a brief pause, he parts our kiss and hovers his fingers over the wet spot.

My breath hitches at the anticipation.

But he doesn't move his hand. Just feels the heat radiating between my legs.

"Please!" I whisper.

His soft eyes flash up to mine before returning to their lingering location under my nightgown. Gently, he presses the pads of his index and middle finger against the sopping fabric. I react like a hysterical virgin who has never been touched. My body writhes in his lap. And to my impending pleasure, Niles releases a satisfied groan.

My clit throbs and pulses as he applies a little more pressure, then pulls his hand away to examine it.

Clear strings of my arousal extend from his fingers to his thumb.

I gasp. "I'm sorry, I'm not normally…"

Not normally what? This wet when I'm near him? When I hear his laugh? When I listen to his jokes? When I feel the warmth of his skin through a fleeting touch?

I am.

Always wet.

To a point of prolonged discomfort.

Niles licks his fingers leisurely, letting his eyes fall closed in euphoria. He hums at the taste, stroking my upper thigh with contained excitement.

"I want to take my time with you," he murmurs in a half-lidded haze. "I don't approach physical intimacy the way most men do. Like animals. Like uncontrollable beasts. I'm patient. I'm gentle. I'm…" He looks up at me through that cloudy thousand-yard stare, "incredibly thorough."

12. Vocation of His Hand

Ruth

"Please, no," I mutter into the dark, chilly room.

After everything on this night, why can't I have a single moment of rest without my life falling to shit? Why can't I suffer the news of Dessin in solitude? Why can't I forget my own burden so I can mourn the loss of my friend?

Warrose left to take a walk in the woods after helping me in bed.

His face drained of all color as he contemplated the idea of life without his oldest friend.

And now it's just me. Here in my new bedroom.

Wet warmth floods between my thighs. Not the good kind. It's the sensation of wetting the bed, yet I know I didn't. My eyes squeeze shut in mute horror before I reach my hand down to the sheets to confirm what the cramping pain in my lower belly is telling me.

Smeared red blots my fingertips.

A twinge of pain forms in my lower back.

Blood.

Cramps.

And I open my mouth to cry out. But instead, I laugh.

"Of course!" I throw my hands up. "What else, right? Hey, why not throw in a sudden fit of diarrhea? Or maybe a stomach bug. I just got news that my best friend is about to suffer for a long, long time. Isn't that enough?"

I laugh again, this time, an angry sputtering laugh.

"And white sheets! *Ha!* Are you having a laugh up there, God?" My eyes burn as the laughter fades. Burn with tears. Burn with resentment. Burn with the inability to blink as I stare at the paint of red across my hand.

A creak ringing from the bedroom doorway snags my attention.

A hulking figure takes up the space. Nothing but a brooding shadow watching me.

"What can I do?" Warrose asks in a thick, rusted-over voice that tells me he's either been yelling into the wind or crying himself hoarse.

I flush with embarrassment. My initial response is to get angry with him, to lash out and tell him to leave. But his face, though hidden in a sheath of shadows, emanates his anguish so clearly.

I don't have the heart to cut him deeper.

"I started my period," I mutter quietly.

Warrose doesn't react, even though I expect some kind of flinch. Aren't men afraid of such things? As a lady, we're taught to never mention our time of bleeding to a man. Ever. It's unseemly. Disgusting. A side of us that should be hidden and tucked away for no one to know about when it's happening.

Warrose doesn't strike me as the type to shy away from the female anatomy in a sense.

And certainly not the type to pale at the sight of blood.

"I have something for that," he finally says. "Will you let me carry you to the washroom to get cleaned up?"

I flush again but nod anyway.

As he shifts into the room with such monstrous grace, I see that his hair is tied back. His loose off-white shirt is open at the chest, revealing his deep bronze skin and dark dusting of hair between his pecs. And his eyes…those dazzling hazel eyes are red-rimmed and so tired. I want to run my fingers under those dark smudges, to heal that look of defeat.

Without examining the blood on the white sheets, or checking my stained nightgown, he waits for me to hook my arm around his neck, then circles his embrace around my body and lifts.

"Are you in pain?" he asks.

Tears sting the backs of my eyes. "Always."

His muscles coil tightly against me, as though his entire frame needs to brace down at the weight of that single word. That terrible sentiment.

He nods once, shifting on his heels and turning to the washroom. The room is lit in a shimmering amber and rose gold from the light of the candles flickering against the copper bathtubs.

Warrose sets me down on a pink velvet chaise lounge, covered in a towel for me to sit on, as he fills the bathtub with hot water.

"What would you like me to add to it?" he asks.

Despite the horror of this situation, I feel a flutter of excitement pass over me.

"Honey, roses, dried lavender, oat milk, and peony salts."

He sifts through cabinets, jars, and glass bottles, pouring and mixing into the steaming copper tub.

"I won't look while you undress."

"Oh." Right. I pull my nightgown over my head slowly, feeling the cool kiss of air brush over my nipples. Quickly, I cover my naked body the best I can as he keeps his promise, preparing the bath for me. There's a full-length mirror against the wall in front of me, and for the first time I look at my reflection.

Protruding collar bones. Jutting rib cage. Dry skin. Thin, dull hair. My *legs*. The stitches. What's happened to me? I hardly recognize myself. The determination to never let Warrose see me naked pumps through my arteries with the ferociousness of a storm.

"I'm going to pick you up, okay? Guide my hands so I don't accidentally touch you in the wrong places." His voice is more gruff than normal. Lower. With an edge of sadness that won't go away. A permanent stain on his tone.

He takes the three steps to me without looking down, lowering his hands down in front of me, palms up to wait for my direction.

My breath gets caught in my throat as I coast his left hand to slide under my bare thighs and the right hand to rest over the middle of my back. Those callouses scratch my soft skin, causing my nipples to pebble and perk up at the sensation.

Why does that have to feel so good? My skin tingles and heats where his hands linger. Chills and goose bumps. A fluttering in my belly. I hold my breath as he clears his throat.

My eyes dance from his pinched brow to the bulging in his pants. *Is he…?*

Warrose lifts me as though I weigh less than air.

And as I sink into the hot, soothing water, I snatch his hand before he can excuse himself.

"Will you stay with me?" I whisper over the tufts of rose-scented steam.

Warrose looks down at me now that the milky water covers my breasts. His heavy, hazel gaze flashes down to my hand gripping his palm, then back up to my pleading look.

"Yes." And it seems as though he's holding in so much pain. So much heartache. Wells of moisture reach my own eyes as I can feel the tangible suffering connecting us tonight.

He sits down on a stool at the side of my tub without pulling his hand away.

"I'm so sorry we've lost Dessin," I breathe thickly.

His jaw goes taut, clenching and unclenching.

"We didn't lose him," he says roughly. "It's Dessin. There's no way–" His voice breaks, and he has to look away.

"What?"

He clears his throat. "There's no way he's not going to fight his way out of this one. There's no way he's going to miss his baby being born. Raising that baby. I won't believe it. My friend has done *impossible* things. He's moved mountains for the woman he loves. Can you imagine what he'd do for his children?" His voice cracks again as he grapples to keep his composure. "We haven't lost him. One way or the other, he'll come back to us."

A trail of warmth permeates through my chest, reaching up to my ears. Deeply embedded resolve dilates his pupils at the notion. And I can't help but release three stray tears.

"I agree. He's too stubborn not to find a way out of this." I nod.

Warrose's lips tilt upward for a heartbeat, and the shadows over his eyes lighten by a single shade.

"And his child will be just as stubborn. Who knows what they'll be capable of? Can you imagine? The product of Patient Thirteen and The Fallen Saint? They're going to give their parents a run for their money. I guarantee you."

I sigh. The faith he has in his best friend. The sheer confidence in his abilities to overcome any obstacle. I feel myself deeply attracted and drawn into that unwavering loyalty.

He is such a good man.

"Thank you for taking care of me," I murmur with watering eyes.

Warrose snaps out of the brief train of thought he was stuck on, sliding his stare down to me with an iron hold on my soul.

"It's no trouble."

"I don't deserve your kindness." I wipe my runny nose with the back of my hand. "I know I've been a headache for you to put up with."

He holds my hand a little tighter. "Don't deserve?" He pauses with an expression that crosses between mortified and disbelief. "Ruth, you deserve more than I could ever give you. But that doesn't mean I won't run myself into the ground every goddamned day to give you more than I did the day before." He shakes his head, looks away, exhales with the slight edge of a growl. "Put up with you? Baby girl, I am enamored by you. I...just want to be around you."

My head falls back as I force myself to take deep, grounding breaths of the steamy air.

Baby girl.

Enamored.

Deserve.

"Okay." I try to smile through the waves of emotions I can't detangle. "That means so much to me. Thank you."

Running a heavy hand through my hair, he sighs. "Wait here. I'm going to change your bedding."

I nearly fall asleep in the hot, sweet-scented water as I wait for Warrose to return.

Something clanks on the countertop behind me, followed by the sound of my name being murmured. A large hand holds out a gold chalice in front of me.

"Skylenna told me this was your favorite."

I blink the sleep away to see a pink liquid inside the gold chalice. Sniffing it, I catch the hint of wine. The sugary kind that most connoisseurs turn their noses up to.

"It is!" I gasp, leveraging my arms to sit up in the tub. "I haven't had this in…what's all this?"

He sets a tray across my tub. It's covered in candy, chocolates, and powdered donuts.

My stomach grumbles right on cue, practically sending small ripples through the milky water. I start to grin. It's the small pull of my lips that lights Warrose's face up.

The beauty of his smile catches me off guard. The fierce point of his brooding stare softens, and the icy blade of his hazel eyes melts for me. It's fair to say that nothing in this world compares to the exquisiteness of his lips stretching over those straight, white teeth with abandon. He's ruggedly handsome, yes. With an edge to his looks, a gruffness that is all man. But *this* smile can only be described as a delicacy. A hidden treasure.

"Look good?" he asks hopefully.

The permeating warmth of that smile flutters through my core.

I nearly burst into tears, nodding my head. "Looks great."

For a while, he sits by my side to read to me while I pick at the sweets and drink until my eyes grow heavy once more, and the buzz of the wine has me fighting to stay awake.

I'm proud of myself for chasing away some of the bad thoughts that come from indulging in desserts. I don't know if they'll ever truly go away. But I'm proud nevertheless.

"I have something else for you once I help you out of the bathtub," he announces, closing the book and reaching for a towel.

"What is it?" I wipe the fog of sleep from my eyes.

"They were at the boutique down main street. I wasn't sure if you've used them ever, but I stocked up on them just in case." Warrose looks away so he can reach into the warm bathwater to lift me. A waterfall pours from my body before he sets me down on the chaise lounge, wrapping my pruned body in a towel big enough to be a small carpet. He never once glances down at me.

"They're feminine inserts. They…" He holds out metal tubes with cotton inside. I lift my chin to examine them.

"Absorb the blood," I finish for him, pink staining my cheeks.

He nods twice.

"I've never used them before." *Always wanted to though.*

"No?"

"No. I've been too scared to try. Kind of feels like trying to give yourself a shot," I say nervously.

Warrose quirks a smile, and it sends a rush straight to my lower belly.

"I could do it for you if you're too scared," he offers without breaking eye contact.

The oxygen is sucked out of the room, and I'm left staring at him with uncertainty.

"Warrose…"

"I don't have to if it makes you uncomfortable. But I just want you to know that it doesn't make *me* uncomfortable. Not in the slightest."

"It doesn't?"

He shakes his head.

I stare at him with my mouth hanging open like an idiot.

"But I've always been under the impression that men are disgusted by…you know. What happens to us every month. We're never supposed to discuss it in mixed company."

His brow furrows. "Anyone disgusted by a woman's body isn't a man."

A single breath gets stuck in my throat.

"Blood or any bodily fluids don't scare me either." His voice goes an octave deeper. "In fact, when I was a teenager, Dessin was about seven or eight, and one night when he slept in my bed with me—he wet the bed. Something scared him the night before in one of his condition treatments. When I woke up, I didn't want to embarrass him, because it was all over me. So I reassured him it was normal and nothing to worry about."

Warrose huffs at the memory. "The little bastard tried to convince me that *I* was the one who wet the bed. And you know him. He was damn good at arguing even then."

I burst out laughing.

"Same situation when he took a nap in my room, had a bad nosebleed, and soaked my pillow. When I confronted him about it, he fully convinced me I had a head wound I didn't know about."

I laugh harder. I suppose little Dessin was just as much as pain in the ass as a child. And Warrose got to experience it all.

"I'm not fazed by blood in the slightest. I spent most of my life in the wild. But if you want to do it alone, I believe you can."

I hum in thought. "I'll do it by myself every other time after this one. Okay?"

I shudder at the notion that I'm growing aroused by this topic. Maybe it's not the act itself of what he's offering to do, but it's certainly the fact that he has no shame. The masculinity to embrace every feminine trait that comes with being a woman is insanely attractive.

I weigh the pros and cons. Am I going to be disgusted with myself if I let him go through with this? Can I just grow a pair and do it myself?

A thrill of exhilaration warps through me unexpectedly.

"I want you to do it," I finally say breathlessly.

His entire bulking posture sits up straight, tall, going stiff and ridged with anticipation. His glittering eyes with long black lashes sweep over me.

"Okay," he exhales.

"Just once. Then I'll do it myself," I add again in a rush.

Butterflies burst from my blood vessels.

I watch Warrose's gaze fall to my inner thighs covered by the large towel.

"I'll be quick," he reassures. And with the slowest movements I've ever seen him make, he lowers himself to his knees in front of me.

I hold my breath.

He clasps the applicator between his two fingers with his thumb resting on the bottom insert. That hulking spartan chest moves up and down as he waits patiently for me to gather the courage to open my legs.

And it's ridiculous, isn't it? How *this* right here is giving me a burst of energy. A triumph of endorphins. I feel in control. I feel like I'm in power. This formidable, muscular man is kneeling for me.

"Okay," I say as I release the breath being held prisoner in my lungs.

My knees part, and my legs open slowly, shifting the towel away to expose myself to him fully. I'm cold and close to shivering, watching his evolving expression with all of my focus.

And his eyes shudder as he swallows. Pupils expand and contract into a dark haze. Eyelids lower into half crests. Jaw locks and flexes repeatedly. He reaches his hand forward to my center, knuckles grazing my inner thigh as he hovers for a moment with uncertainty.

"May I?" he asks in a rasping voice.

"Yes." Hardly a whisper.

He breathes in deeply through his nose, then uses two fingers to spread my lips and line up the applicator. My entire body seems to gulp at the sensation. Hot lava pours into my lower belly. I fight to keep my composure, not letting him know how much this turns me on. His fingers so close to my throbbing clit. Yet he's all business. No signs of arousal for him.

The tip of the applicator adds pressure to my opening before he slides it inside me.

At this, I can't help but gasp, and like a clap of thunder, his darkened gaze shoots up to my face. His pause is brief but filled with a boiling tension.

He injects the absorbent cotton with ease, and I hardly notice a sensation from it until he pulls the metal out of my center, leaving my opening quivering at its loss.

Why am I out of breath?

"How…" Warrose swallows, closing his eyes for a moment. "How does that feel?"

Like I could have an orgasm if you just touched me a little more…

"Fine. Good. Yeah." I throw the towel back over my lap. "It didn't hurt at all."

Warrose's hazel eyes flick back and forth between mine as he tries to analyze something, a question, a topic of conversation in his mind. Instead of voicing it, he settles on a nod.

But as I break eye contact, my eyes land on his pants again. He's…hard. The full outline of his cock is on display. Should I do something? Is he experiencing the same feelings I am? Could we find what we lost in the prison?

"Your bed is made, and I started another fire. I'll get you a new nightgown too," he says.

"No," I blurt out.

Warrose stops mid-turn on his heels.

Should I make this move or not?

"I want to sleep naked tonight."

He does a double take.

What am I doing? Flirting? Am I rusty, or is it working?

"You do…"

"Yes." I look up at him from under my eyelashes. But I want to laugh. Damn, Skylenna would definitely laugh at this attempt. Couldn't I have transitioned that a little better?

His lips part, and for a heartbeat, his eyes fall to my body covered in this towel, like he's thinking about it. Like he's imagining what I'll look like.

His nod is clipped and stern. "Alright. I'll let you get to it then."

What?!

He's careful as he lifts me off the pink velvet seat, carrying me back to bed. I sink into the mattress as he lays my hair on a towel so it doesn't get my pillow wet. The sheets smell of honey and vanilla. Fresh. Clean. Warm.

As he takes a step away from my bed, I yank the damp towel from my body and toss it at his feet. The heavy, white comforter covers just above the swell of my breasts.

His eyes dart down to the towel, then back up to me.

I watch him carefully.

This is it…

But my stomach rolls over, then sinks into a shallow grave as Warrose picks up the towel to hang up. *Please, please don't do this.* I need to feel beautiful right now. I need to feel sexy.

"I'll let you get some sleep," he murmurs roughly.

My bones ache at those six words. Everything seems to wilt on impact. So, it's true then… His attraction ended for me with that last kiss we shared before I took his punishment in prison.

It dawns on me.

I took his punishment.

My legs were a sacrifice for him.

For my friends.

Everything inside me is sucked into a black, cold pit. My bones are chilled. My heart is molting like an old bird.

He's staying by my side out of guilt. Of course, he isn't attracted to me. How could he be? Look at me! I'm a shell of the woman I was before all of this.

God, did I throw myself at him tonight? How could I be so stupidly hopeful? So blind?

He's a good man acting out of duty. Nothing more. Sure, he enjoys me as a friend, yes. But that deep chemistry was chopped away from us when the axe fell, wasn't it?

My eyes burn but I refuse to cry.

Shame.

Embarrassment.

Hopelessness.

Misery.

I guess Niles was wrong. Not all of us get to have a soul mate.

13. She is a Lion

Marilynn

Niles slides his hand over my thigh as the debate grows louder within the Demechnef council.

It is a roundtable full of old White men.

All men.

Men.

Men.

Men.

It's the final meeting on who will take Aurick Demechnef's place as leader. Though it shouldn't be a discussion, should it? After all, the former name of this government was Demechforth. A combination of Blackforth and Demechnef. There have always been *two* leaders in this country. My family's name was blackened from future plans here.

Blackforth.

"I vote *I* take Aurick's place until the baby turns twenty-five. It's what Aurick would have wanted!" Ratticus taps his fingers on the cherrywood table in emphasis.

He's the most outspoken member of this board. Dark gray, wispy hair. Sunspots all over his chubby face. Smoke lines around his mouth. Globs of spittle gathering at the corners of his mouth when he speaks.

I remain quiet. Still. Watchful.

Niles, on the other hand, is having trouble sitting still, keeping his mouth shut.

But he knows I only let him come if he promised to stay silent.

"Not a very good argument, Ratticus. I think Mr. Demechnef would have wanted Ms. Blackforth to, at the very least, act as regent until the baby turned of age…" Otis sips his coffee with a look of boredom stretching over his sleepy blue eyes.

My last name is Blackforth.

Fuck my ties to Aurick Demechnef.

Blackforth.

Blackforth.

Blackforth.

My right.

"She's a *woman*," the old man at the opposite end of the table says with a scowl.

Niles grips my thigh harder.

"Right, Nevil! A woman leading Demechnef. Can you imagine?" Ratticus chokes out a laugh, spraying saliva across the table. "What next? No more lady-doll regimens?"

The table breaks out in a fit of chuckles.

"Is that such a frightening thought, gentlemen?" I break my silence.

Niles goes stiff as he turns to watch me *unfold.*

"What's that, *girl?*" Ratticus cringes.

"The abolishment of the lady-doll regimen." I pause, savoring the way their faces warp in disgust. "Giving the women of Demechnef agency over their own bodies again."

"It's an absurd idea that has no shot in hell of ever happening, yes." Nevil sits up straighter.

"Hmm." I nod to myself, fighting the urge to smile. "I think I'd like to make it happen. Effective immediately."

I can tell Niles wants to ask me what the hell I'm doing. That this isn't the way to convince a roundtable full of misogynistic white men that they should give leadership over to me. A *woman.*

"Even more reason to make me regent. I won't be changing anything!" Ratticus continues to campaign.

I've prepared for this moment my entire life.

The name Blackforth was abolished from being mentioned again due to Aurick's father, Vlademur Demechnef. He poisoned my father, Gregory, at a party several years ago for changing his stance on the way this country was run. My mother brought him to the asylum, forcing him to observe the force-feedings of lady-doll regimen victims. She spent much time educating him on the oppression of women, helping him understand that those morals are wrong. Evil. *Obscene.*

After he voiced to the council to change the laws that hurt the women of our country, Vlademur slipped arsenic in his champagne. Then proceeded to attack my mother in a fit of rage for taking his best friend away from him, altering his mind with her insidious, feminine ways of persuasion.

Later that evening, he tied her body to the back of his buggy and dragged her through the cobblestone streets for three miles.

Judas and I buried her next to our father in the Red Oaks, where our people gathered without being told, holding candles and humming a song we only sing when there's a death among us.

I vowed to Judas that day I wouldn't let them down when the time came.

I pass around a sealed envelope. "Before Aurick showed up at the Vexeman border to war, he wrote out a will in case anything should happen to him."

I've contemplated burning the will. This role is mine without his support.

Otis opens the envelope, reads quickly, then looks up at his fellow board members in surprise. "It says Marilynn Blackforth should receive his entire inheritance, estates, and position as leader of Demechnef if he should perish."

Despite my need to have this on my own, gratitude crumples my heart into a somber wad.

"That's probably doctored! Gentlemen, please! Aurick Demechnef would never give rule to a fucking woman!" With that, Ratticus tosses the will into the fireplace, then his glass of whiskey to make the fire explode into the chimney.

Niles slams his hands down. "Hey!"

I snag his wrist, urging him to remain calm no matter what. Does he think I didn't know this would happen?

Nothing about this day will surprise me.

I rise from my seat with thirteen files in my hands, relishing this moment before impact.

"I anticipated you'd all think so little of me. Doctoring the will of the leader of this country." I toss the files in the center of the table, letting the men grab their own.

"In fact…my family, generations back, has anticipated this day for a very long time. They anticipated a room full of entitled men would attempt to deny me the opportunity to making this country a better place for my child."

Niles gawks up at me, watching the show with a look of bewilderment and admiration.

"So, as you can see with the titles in those files. The Blackforth name owns the majority of land in Dementia. I own the Delilian Castle. I own the land your estates sit on. I own every inch aside from the seven forests and the Bear Traps. I could evict you all without a second thought. Where would you go then? The Evergreen Dark Wood? The colony of that region isn't exactly fond of your kind there. The shores of Vexamen? You see, my family comes from a long lineage from the ancient colony of the Crimson Kres of the Red Oaks. If you deny me my birthright, I've already assembled the seven colonies to bear arms against you."

"You dare plan a hostile takeover!" Nevil hisses.

"Why don't you sit on your ass and wait to see if I do?" I smile with malice and cold, contained rage. "Because I couldn't possibly be capable of such a thing, could I? I am a woman. Isn't that right? Women. Can't. Lead."

The room is cocooned in a wave of silence and disbelief.

"Well, you can choose to stand with this woman or watch this woman burn your homes to the ground. Your choice."

14. The Wooden Throne

Ruth

"The sun hasn't even come up yet!"

I squirm as Warrose layers me in coats, mittens, a knitted hat that covers my ears, two fluffy scarfs, and leg warmers.

"Here." He hands me a pink porcelain thermos. The opening smells of cinnamon and chocolate. "It's coffee with frothed oat milk, sweet cream, and melted chocolate candies. You can drink it on the way."

My heart turns to mush. He's so thoughtful. I wish to God he didn't feel this obligation. It makes me feel guilty. Ugly. A pungent burden that lingers.

"Why? Where are we going?"

"It's a surprise." His morning voice is scratchy, baritone deep, and devastating.

"A surprise?"

Warrose gently tucks my hair behind my ears, studying my face with calm thoughtfulness. "Mm-hmm."

A buggy takes us to the edge of the North Sapphrine Forest, a hidden nook of thick evergreen trees covered in snowflakes and red berries. And as we get out of the buggy, the sunrise peaks over the mountains, bleeding through the blueish-green needles of the white spruce.

I breathe in the scent of winter pine, snow, and the steam of my sweet coffee.

Warrose adjusts me in his arms, cradling me close to his chest for warmth.

"What's going on?" I ask.

"I've been working really hard on something," he replies.

I peer around as he walks us deeper into the enchanted nook of forest. A small clearing next to a babbling brook somehow escaped the freeze.

"You see those three trees?" He points a few feet ahead.

I squint my eyes. "There are only two and a stump."

But my, those two do look out of place. They're a stunning mix between evergreen and a wild maple tree. Wide twisted branches, fluffy pine needles that sparkle like diamonds in the morning sun, and the rich scent of eucalyptus.

"They're called Delilian's Hearts," he explains. "There's a legend among the colonies that these trees are fireproof. They've stood for thousands of years, through wildfires, storms, and war. It's said that they were created by ancient time travelers."

Wow. I crank my neck to glance up at their towering heights.

"Where did the third one go?" I ask.

"I cut it down."

"You what?!"

Warrose sets me down on a large stone mounting out of the snowy earth. He walks around the two trees, hidden by shadows and their long underbrush.

"I made this for you." He pushes a giant chair out from around the trees. It glides easily with wheels over the snow and roots.

I sit up straighter.

"It took me a long time to carve it. This wood is damn near

impervious. But with these wheels, you won't need anyone to get where you want to go. You'll have power over taking care of yourself if you wish from now on." He fidgets with the handles. "The inside of the seat I had custom made down at the corner boutique. It's really soft, like sitting on a cloud."

My mouth falls open as I examine it.

"Bring it closer," I mutter.

As he rolls it a couple feet away from me, I notice the exquisite design etched into the wood, molded and carved to perfection.

Animals. He carved animals.

The wood is glossy and dark, so brown it could pass for black. It enhances the intricate details in the heads of the animals over the trim of the rolling chair.

"You carved all of that?" I say, nearly speechless. My thoughts disappear before they're formed.

"Yes."

"What kind of animals are these?"

Warrose takes a seat next to me, looking out at the enchanted nook, as if he's trying to spot something. "Have you ever heard of the Winter Storm Lions?"

I shake my head.

"They're a rare pack of lions native to the North Sapphrine Forest. Very resilient. Fierce. But it's said they have an unmatched compass for good-hearted humans." He whistles into the distance, blowing foggy air into the cold. "That's why they fought with us in Vexamen. They not only followed DaiSzek into battle…"

A branch snaps behind the Delilian Heart trees. I turn my head, following Warrose's focused stare. Creeping out from the underbrush emerges a beautiful white lion, fur long and glittering like the dewy snow. Eyes pale blue with a luscious mane and small horns at the top of its head.

Fear strikes like a lightning bolt in my gut.

"War-rose…" I tap him on the shoulder in alarm.

"Look." He smiles.

Several others appear in the hidden nook, surrounding us.

"Oh god," I gasp. "We're being hunted!"

"I called them." He chuckles. "Look closer, little rebel."

I clutch his arm, still unsure of our situation, but do as he says. I focus on the first Winter Storm Lion approaching, study the details of…

"*Wait*," I utter.

"Mm-hmm."

Its back left leg is gone. I look to the next lion. Missing eye. And the one after that, no ears. They are all maimed and missing a part of themselves.

"What happened to them?"

"They eliminated threats against DaiSzek in battle. They fought packs of Vexamen Garbucks ten to one. They were outnumbered but fought like hell to protect the king."

"What are Garbucks? And…DaiSzek is a king?"

Warrose nods. "A venomous lion native to Vexamen. And yes, to them he is a king."

I grow eerily quiet as I watch them walk closer. Despite missing legs, some paws, they shift their weight when they walk, balancing with each step. Even behind their fur I can see how muscular they are. Contours of their lean, cut definition.

"Are you okay if they approach?" he asks, voice like a crackling fire and a searing flame.

I take another sip of my coffee and lick my lips. Nod twice. My hands twitch and tremble with nerves and the shrill bite of the icy wind.

Don't be afraid. You've been around DaiSzek, and he's the most terrifying beast there is.

Warrose motions to the majestic beasts with his hand, and their ears perk up at the invitation. Watching them close in on me is like standing under a tidal wave, waiting for it to come crashing down overhead.

I stay perfectly still. Unable to look away from their piercing blades of ice for eyes.

The one that appeared first takes two more steps to come near eye level with me, huffing cold puffs of fog, pink nostrils flaring as it studies my scent.

"What do I do?" I release an anxious breath.

"Let go of your nerves, little rebel. Winter Storm Lions detect emotions the way night dawpers smell blood. Let her in…"

And it's something about the warmth of his voice paired with the gentle patience of the lion's icy eyes. She hovers over my lap, watching me, waiting.

I turn my palms upward on my thighs, opening them to the underside of her face.

They detect emotions.

The quiet lion lowers her chin into my hands, slowly, carefully.

What emotions must she feel from me?

Those sweet arctic eyes gloss over with tears.

The sight of it pierces my heart, leaving my knees throbbing and sore at the memory of the axe. The blood loss after it happened. The feeling of Dessin sawing and sewing, fighting to save my life. The sickness that followed. The fever. The nausea. The hopelessness. The terror of being left to rot in that prison alone.

My chest feels raw and heavy, and I look up at Warrose to my right, blinking against the hot well of tears rising in my eyes.

His face contorts into a look of calm anguish. "Remember when I told you that when we finally left the prison, I'd take you somewhere safe?"

I nod, holding myself together.

"Somewhere you could let yourself fall to pieces?" he rasps.

Tears bulge over my eyes to the point of pressurized pain.

His fingers graze my flushed cheek tenderly. "I promise to mix my pieces with yours, baby girl. You can fall now."

The wet sadness streams from my eyes to the edge of my jaw. And as I turn to look back down at the lion, she burrows into my hands and legs, pressing her sympathy and comfort deeply against me.

My sob erupts out of my lungs followed by an achy, unrelenting throb in my chest. It isn't soft. It isn't a gentle whimper. The cry that breaks free is loud, guttural, *tortured.* It's a howl of agony that scrapes up against my esophagus, ricocheting across the snow and the icicles and the bubbling surface of the babbling brook.

And Warrose watches me catch flame with dark eyebrows that knit together in silent suffering. He winces as my cry swirls into a scream, then back to a moaning howl.

"They took my legs!" I bellow.

I'm certain that my sudden outburst will scare away the pack of glittering white lions. But oddly enough, they are attracted to the noise. One by one, they gather closer, nuzzling against my back, my arms, climbing onto the rock to burrow into the nape of my neck.

"I know," Warrose replies thickly.

"I want to run again!" I wail, leaning against the lion to my left. "I'm broken! I'm useless! I fucking hate myself!"

At this, Warrose's giant hand swallows the back of my neck in his calloused grip.

"Please don't say that!" he says gruffly against the side of my head. "God, please never say that again."

I shake my head repeatedly. The grief I feel for this loss is spreading toxic webs deep down in a dark, chilled place within myself. My gushing eyes drop down to my legs. Oh, how my heart is bludgeoned every time I look at their new length. And every morning I wake, my chest leaps with a galloping thump of hope that it was all a nightmare.

But my *life* is the nightmare now.

"I just want to die! I-I want this all to be over!" I cry harder, feeling the lions warm the chill in my bones as they form a cocoon around Warrose and me. "I don't feel beautiful anymore. I don't feel strong. I wish I would have died on that post!"

I turn to glance at Warrose, but the moment isn't fleeting. I catch the trails of shine down his cheeks. With bloodshot eyes, he shakes his head. Dumbfounded by my confession.

"Fucking hell, Ruth. You are the most stunning woman I've ever laid my eyes on. Your features aren't from this world. They're diamonds to specks of sand. I can't look away, even though seeing you in pain physically wounds me."

I open my mouth to respond with more self-deprecating words. But he isn't finished.

"And strength? Most wouldn't have survived what you've endured. You are far stronger now than you were when we entered that godforsaken place. You're a born leader who now knows great suffering and deep-rooted grief." He traps my face in his warm, rough hands, catching my tears as they fall. And gently, he rests his forehead against mine, tickling my lips with his winter breath.

"I feel so helpless," I whisper.

"Just for now. In time, you'll heal both mind and body. You'll thrive." He kisses the tip of my nose, sending a shock through my spine.

I squeeze my eyes shut, pushing out more tears. I want to believe that so badly. I want to move past this. I want to be happy again.

"But…" I feel silly for asking this. "You find me so beautiful, yet you're not attracted to me?"

My stomach twists with anticipation. I'm not sure I'm ready for this answer. Not sure I'm ready to watch him find the words to let me down easy.

Though my vision is blurry, I could swear I notice the corner of his mouth curl upward.

"You think I'm not attracted to you?" An eyebrow raises. Warrose, with his forehead still pressed against mine, leans in again to graze his lips over my cheekbone. And again to place a warm kiss a fraction of an inch away from the corner of my mouth. Tingles pass over my nervous system as I melt.

I nod with embarrassment darkening my cheeks and contracting my muscles.

As Warrose parts his lips, searching for the right words to puncture my heart gently, a swell of storm clouds stretches across the sky followed by epic forks of purple lightning, and fervent claps of thunder.

"We need to go now," he says.

I give sobbing, sweet kisses on the heads of the lions before we leave them. I had no idea that the kind of unwavering affection of an animal is what I needed to let go. That soft fur. Those patient, light blue eyes. They sacrificed parts of their body too for the cause of saving another.

As Warrose sets me down on my new chair, I feel both depressed and liberated.

He walks behind me as I use the wheels to roll myself across the snow.

But after a few yards, my arms tremble with exhaustion. Muscles burning like hell fire as I try to push through it and hit my destination of that buggy waiting for us to come back.

I move slower and slower, barely covering inches of snow with the speed I'm going.

"Here, I can push you the rest of the way," Warrose says, gripping the handlebars behind me.

"No!" I pant, cranking my head to look back at him. "I want to do this myself."

Sweat streams down my temples despite the crisp winds.

"You got it," he responds, taking a step away. "You're going slightly uphill. I'll be right behind you if you need me, okay?"

I nod, unable to speak through the labored breathing.

Clenching and unclenching my hands around the handlebars of the wheels, I strain my eyes through the snow now falling from the smoky storm clouds overhead. The buggy is in sight now, glimmering in a small ray of sun that's bleeding through an opening of clouds.

You're going slightly uphill.

I'll need to push harder and faster, bulldozing through the soreness and fatigue to get past this incline. I can do this. Pain is no stranger to me. I can fight through anything that ails my body. After undergoing surgery in the coed bathrooms of a barbaric prison, awake and bleeding out, I can overcome anything.

Huffing a final breath through my nose, I begin shoving those wheels forward with all my strength, one push at a time, gritting my teeth through the fire beaming up my arms.

"Almost there," Warrose encourages behind me.

I grunt at the next push forward, barely making any leeway at all. My bones feel battered and swollen. My hands are locking up and going stiff from gripping too hard.

"Damnit." I shake my head, unable to catch my breath.

I'm too weak. I've been lying in a bed without any physical activity for too long.

"Talk to me," Warrose calls from a few feet behind me.

"I can't..." *Too tired. Too weak.*

"Can't what?" he asks. "Can't talk or can't make it to the buggy?"

"B-both."

I hear the crunching of Warrose's boots through the snow. His towering, wide frame appears to my left. Shoulders and black hair covered in snowflakes.

"In time, you're going to strengthen your body, okay? But right now, it's about mental toughness. Your mind is strong enough to command your body to do impossible things." He touches my chin. "Hey, look at me. If you want to stop, I'll push you the rest of the way. But I know for a fact that if you can make it a few more yards, you'll feel fucking amazing the rest of the day."

"I w-will?" *Can't breathe. Can't think.*

He narrows his shimmery hazel eyes on me, seeping into the pit of my soul.

"You need a win, little rebel. Let this be your first."

Hope seeps within a hidden nook of my heart. I do need a win. I need something to look forward to. I need *this* win.

"Okay. But I n-need you to talk to me," I huff, readjusting my grip on the wheels.

Warrose nods fiercely. "I want you to remember things that pump adrenaline into your body, okay? Remember when we were running through the dunes and pits, away from the Vexamen army."

I think back to that day. When Warrose fell from the blast of a bomb, falling down the side of a cliff, and using his bare back to slide down the rocky path so I wouldn't get hurt. He tried to muffle his roar, his groans, his screams. But it was agony for him.

Fire pumps through my veins at the thought, and I push two times with numb, shaking arms.

"Remember watching Skylenna ride DaiSzek into battle, standing on the length of his spine, tilting her head back as he breathed fire to the front line of the army."

My skin tingles head to toe. I haven't thought about that moment since the day it happened. I felt the pure, uncontained heat of his fire. The tendrils of yellow, orange, and red. It was a masterpiece from both of them.

I'm elated at the thought. More strength pours into me as I grunt, bucking my entire body to roll faster, ignoring the way my entire back clenches and contracts in aching distress.

"And remember the day you made it to the buggy without any help," Warrose says softly.

He steps out of my line of sight, revealing the buggy door, open and waiting for me.

I start to cry.

"I-I made it!" I squeal. So many tears. Dripping. Soaking my coat.

"You fucking made it, baby girl!" Warrose lifts me from my seat, hugging me to his chest while spinning us in a circle.

I go limp, a pile of putty in his arms. But I've never felt better in all my life. Euphoria soars like a sky of ravens through my nervous system. And I cry and laugh against his shoulder.

"I MADE IT!" I scream into the stormy winds.

Snow falls around us, reminding me of the final moments after the battle in Vexamen. When DaiSzek crawled over Knightingale's ashes, whimpering for the loss of his dear friend. That brave little soul who sacrificed without another thought.

It's a reminder. The war is over. And I survived.

I made it.

15. "Please wake up."

Skylenna

"**K**ane! I made us cookies! I'm going to eat them all unless you get out of the water and come sit with me right this second!"

I watch an eight-year-old Skylenna scream over the cliff of the lagoon holding a plate of snickerdoodles. It's the middle of summer, and Kane went for a swim the moment they arrived at the Red Oaks. Skylenna made lemonade, cookies, and set up a picnic for them while he worked out his frustrations in the water.

"KANE!" Young Skylenna shrieks with balled fists and a red face.

My heart corkscrews in a fit of pain as I hear…his *laugh*.

"You have as much patience as a monsoon, Skylittle." Kane chuckles, climbing up and around the bank to come back to her.

"I made these special for you, and yet you'd rather be swimming!"

"I'm here, I'm here."

But she didn't see it, did she?

The bruises on his neck. They look like the imprint of someone's hands. I can't imagine the other marks that will reveal themselves underneath his clothes. There's a reason he wouldn't take his shirt off to swim.

I sit behind them, watching the two children eat the snickerdoodles, drink their lemonade, and bask in the hot summer sun. They swim for hours. Laugh and tell stories. And then when the sun starts to set, Kane makes a fire, and young Skylenna falls asleep on his chest.

I watch it all with a numbness that spreads unevenly through my vascular system.

"Skylenna," a scratchy voice calls through the void.

Pressure swells behind my eyes as I want to cry taking one last look at them. Envy. Bitterness. Sorrow. Hopelessness. Intense longing. I wish I could tell them every pitfall to watch out for. Tell them how to escape to find a better life. Tell them to find the island where Knightingale and DaiSzek never got to live out the ends of their lives together.

I return from the void, sitting on the porch Kane and I built together, staring out at the lagoon with a clenched jaw and tired eyes.

"You're cold to the touch, child." Chekiss folds a blanket over my shoulders, rubbing his hands up and down my arms. "I think you were in the void too long again."

Not long enough.

DaiSzek whimpers in my lap, using his heavy head to warm my lower body.

I peer up at the sky beyond the awning of the porch to see how long I've been under. It was this morning with my coffee when I decided to return to the days under the sun, where life was happier when I had my best friend.

The stars are sprinkled across the sky now. Pin holes of tiny white lights, like glitter and glowing coals among the vast blackness of midnight.

"I made you supper if you're hungry…" Chekiss adds, concern lowering his voice to a harsh whisper.

My stomach ripples with a deep groan.

I nod.

My bladder is full too. And I can't seem to get warm.

"I made a fire, gathered a few fur blankets. You can get warm while you eat," he adds.

I place a small kiss on his hand. "Thank you."

After relieving myself, I sit on a pile of pillows in front of the fireplace, wrapped in fur blankets, while eating a bowl of soup. Chekiss and DaiSzek eat next to me.

"You can talk to me, you know," Chekiss says between bites. "I know I'm not much, but I can listen. And sometimes it's good to get things off your chest."

I peer over at him. "You *are* much. You mean the world to me."

His smile is filled with quiet grief.

I set my bowl down. "I'm starting to think that being a warrior angel is a curse God gave to those who must have made grave sins in a past life."

Chekiss watches me with a patient stillness about him.

"DaiSzek and Knightingale never made it to their quiet, peaceful life they always wanted. They were martyrs. Dessin and I are no different. Death would have been better than this, wouldn't it? I'm pregnant! And I may never see him again. He may never meet his baby. How could this happen? How could God be this cruel?"

I don't cry when speaking on such heavy topics. Asking such damning questions. How can I? I have no tears left to give.

Chekiss shakes his head, feeling as lost and helpless as I've been feeling since the moment Kaspias gave me this news.

"All I want is for him to wake up and hold me. For him to show up and shock everyone the way he's always done. But I can't even find him in the void. I've searched until my body nearly gave out from hypothermia." DaiSzek places his head back onto my lap. "I miss his voice. His laugh. The way his face twists with annoyance when Niles talks."

We both chuckle.

"I miss how sweet he was to me and cruel to everyone else."

"Not everyone," Chekiss interjects. "Most, yes. But even though he acted otherwise, I know he loved all of us too. He protected his family until the very end."

My chest rises with that familiar stabbing sensation of grief. I look over my shoulder at the dark hallway, feeling both yearning in my chest and the need to avoid going to our bedroom where he rests.

The love of my life is connected to wires and tubes to help him breathe and continue getting nutrition. Is it inhumane to help keep him alive when we know he won't be waking up? Maybe for anyone else. But for Dessin?

There is always a chance.

"Did you know there were two other test subjects before us in the experiment? Different abilities like Dessin and me."

Chekiss shakes his head.

"Dessin told me about it once when we were on the run. Val and Vinaley. Through his trauma, Val had the ability to uncover anyone's greatest fears and capitalize on them. No one knew what Vinaley could do because she had retreated so far into herself." I feel a rush of longing, remembering Dessin telling me all of this by the fire he built. "He loved her, though. And in the end, she couldn't take the trauma anymore. She ended her life…and he was right behind her."

DaiSzek finishes his large bowl of food that Chekiss made him and lays his head on my lap, sensing that I'm holding myself together talking about this.

"I guess that's an occupational hazard, huh? Those of us who were thrown into the experiment together aren't much without the other," I say quietly.

"Skylenna…" Chekiss scolds, giving me that stern look only a father can give.

I chuckle sadly. "Don't worry, I'm not going to hurt myself. I have his baby to take care of. I'm just saying, my quality of life isn't much anymore now."

With a frail hand on my shoulder, he says, "Just wait until you give birth, child. You're empty now, yes. But once you see that little life in her arms for the first time, you've never known a love like that. And no one is going to love you like your baby." He pauses, then widens his eyes. "Or *babies*."

"Plural?" I wince.

"Twins run in both of your families." He shrugs.

I shake my head. "Yeah but…unlikely."

"No need to think about that now. You still have a long way to go."

I haven't given much thought to this pregnancy or the baby. What they'll look like. Names. If they'll have my eyes or Dessin's. Emerald green or chocolate brown. If they'll be sweet like Kane or calculated like Dessin. It feels like driving a rusted screw through my chest cavity to give into these fantasies. Because he's not here to dream about it with me. Kane isn't here to take care of me through the morning sickness, cramping, headaches, nasal congestion, extreme exhaustion. It's just me, Chekiss, and my sweet, wounded DaiSzek.

I take one last look down that daunting hallway.

"I think I'll sleep on the couch again tonight," I mutter.

Chekiss rubs my shoulder, humming his agreement. And as he leaves to get me clothes to sleep in and pillows for the couch, I stare into that fire, pretending I'm back under the trees with him. On the run. Surviving in the forest together.

I'd take that life over this one.

War and all.

At least we were together.

16. The Road Home

Marilynn

"You really fucked up that board of geriatric patients, huh?" Niles comments as we walk back to the buggy waiting for us on the side of the mountain.

I laugh.

"Seriously, you were a marvel to witness," he adds.

We follow behind a few men carrying boxes of paperwork, files, reports, and important documents I have to sign when I get home. They pile them in the passenger seat and two-thirds of the back seat.

Niles and I stare at the one open seat, then turn to look at each other.

"I can walk home. You go ahead," he insists, patting my back to enter the buggy without him.

I scoff. "Am I too heavy to sit on your lap then?"

He scoffs louder, practically throwing himself in the seat and patting his lap in invitation for me to sit down. He grins.

"I know my thighs have a lot of muscle, but don't be intimidated. They make a very comfortable chair."

I roll my eyes and smirk away from him. I haven't heard his humor a whole lot lately. I wonder if it's because he uses it as a shield when he's in danger or nervous. A trauma response.

Is he nervous now?

As I lower myself into his lap, I watch his face in the rearview mirror. His expression loses all color of humor. And he seems to hold his breath as his eyes lower to my backside pressing against his lap to get adjusted.

Yes, definitely nervous.

A rush of heat splashes in my lower belly at the contact.

"Is *this* okay?" I ask.

At least three seconds of silence.

"Yes."

I hold my breath as the buggy begins moving.

Surprisingly, Niles keeps his hands firmly at his sides. It makes me a little self-conscious, so I cross my arms over my chest.

Clunk, clunk... Clunk!

The buggy drives over rocky, uneven terrain that jostles me in my seat. I hit my head on the ceiling, then bump my right shoulder into the window.

"*Arg!*" I hiss.

Niles instinctually grips the soft space where my hips meet my thighs. His fingers slip into the crease as I try to readjust myself.

"Sorry! It's rough getting out of here!" the driver calls.

We ignore him. My thoughts are blistering with the outrageous tingling sensation where his hands meet my thighs. He holds me in place, stroking the pads of his index fingers over my dress. I nearly black out at the touch.

"Relax," Niles breathes against my neck. "I'm not going to let go."

Violent shivers roll down my spine.

I exhale quickly. "Thank you."

"Mm-hmm."

I'm beyond desperate to touch him back. To stir something inside of him the way it's been raging inside me. My hand hovers over his before I gently let it settle over his knuckles, caressing up and down from fingertips to wrist.

His hands coil around my skin tighter, like a snake tightening around its prey.

The jostling buggy sends my body bouncing on his lap, and I don't know what comes over me…but a needy animal awakens in the pit of my stomach, purring and frenzied with scandalous thoughts. I arch my back with each jolt, rolling my ass against his crotch as if it's all a subtle accident. An innocent reaction to the bumpy road ahead.

Stop it. It's too easy to want him.

Niles tightens the rigid muscles in his abdomen that are pressed to my back. His breath hitches as I keep up with the jerky movement. After a moment of doubt, I feel him rise against my backside. His erection is stone against the softness of my ass, making me ache to touch it, to feel it pulse against my center.

He hesitates before shifting his hands from my hips, gliding them to my inner thighs. It lights me up, a blazing flame of desire singes through my lower body. The fevered pulse in my clit causes my opening to contract repeatedly, frantic to be filled by him.

This is crazy. You're in a moving buggy with a driver in the car!

I roll my hips again, this time quite intentional without the guise of an accident from the jostling buggy. My ass rubs firmly against his thickness, eliciting a faint grunt of pleasure from his lips.

His hands shift again, this time to where my tender inner thighs meet the lips of my pussy. The spot that's almost ticklish at unexpected contact that isn't from my own fingers. It drives me up a wall as he tests his boundaries by massaging me, then grazing my lips covered by my panties with the backs of his fingers (as if by accident).

I tremble as my wetness leaks.

"Are you comfortable?" Niles murmurs against the back of my neck as if the intimacy happening isn't actually happening.

"Uh-huh." My exhale is long and drawn out, coming close to a moan.

"Good." He uses the pad of his middle finger to nudge and massage the center of my panties, barely touching the wet slit that exposes my clit under the fabric.

I'm throbbing and soaking through on his finger.

He inhales sharply through his nose.

With another bump on the road, I'm flush against his chest, melting into the hard lines of his body. His scent of fresh linens, soap, and pure sunshine is warping my mind in terrible, lovely ways. I suddenly want to spill all my secrets, tell him everything I know, bear my soul to him.

To make matters worse, Niles slowly tugs my panties to the side, gliding two fingers across my gushing arousal. I don't know whether to be embarrassed or excited as he uses it to add a little more glossy pressure to my sensitive bundle of nerves. Kneading and working gently, until I'm heavy breathing through my nose, trying not to alert the driver that I'm going insane in his backseat.

"You're squirming," Niles comments. "Want me to help keep you still?"

I gulp loud enough for the entire city to hear and nod eagerly.

I expect his arms to wrap around my center, holding me tightly until the ride is over. The thought and visual image disappoints me greatly.

But Niles unzips his pants, lifts my hips until he's lined up with my center, the tip of his cock inching my panties to the side. His head is nudging my entrance.

I suck in a sharp breath through my teeth.

"*Oh*," I coo, looking up at the rearview mirror at the driver to see his eyes cluelessly on the road. My hazy eyes peer back at Niles.

Heavens, he's a sight to see. Beautiful. Stunning. Fine, golden hair that looks wind-blown and styled. Downturned eyes that seem to fade from a teal to blue. His soft lips are parted, finally showing signs of being disheveled by me for once.

"Is this okay?" he asks, though it isn't exactly Niles's voice. It's something close. Rougher. Strained. Containing unseen pressure.

"Yes."

"What about now?"

He lowers my hips to push the head of his cock into my slick entrance.

We both make noises that resemble a cross between hissing and a strangled groan. My core lights on fire, pleasure jutting through my nerves until I feel blind with shock.

"You can say no, my love. I'll stop."

My love.

My love.

My love.

My eyes water.

I shake my head. "Just go slow. I want this."

I want to savor it. To remember it for the rest of my life.

Niles's chest expands as he breathes deeply, placing a small kiss on my shoulder blade, then lowering me another inch.

Lust fills my bloodstream like a drug. *Holy shit.*

Another inch.

He lets his head fall against my back, panting against my dress. And I gush around him, lubricating his shaft as it glides inside me a little more.

"No further," Niles whispers between his panting breaths. "The first time I push myself all the way inside you will be the first time I lay you down and make love to you."

I clench around the head of his cock.

Niles hums his pleasure.

Make love to you.

"I'd like that," I say quietly.

I clench and unclench around him again, causing a chemical reaction in my lower belly. I'm radiating with bottled pleasure, swallowing me whole with each second that passes swiftly.

"I've never had this much trouble lasting," Niles breathes.

"What do you mean?"

"I mean, I'm fighting for my life over here not to come inside you."

He sounds so serious. So unlike himself with a tint of frustration and euphoria warping his tone. My hands lock around his wrists to get his attention.

"So don't," I say boldly. "Tonight, you're going to lay me down, hold my legs over my head, and angle your dick to go as deep inside of me as you want when you make love to me."

I tilt my head to see Niles looking absolutely baffled.

Another bump on the road has us both struggling to keep me from sliding all the way down his shaft.

"I'll make it so special, Mar. Leave everything to me."

And I believe it. Truly, to the pit of my soul. It's Niles Offborth. The golden boy with sunshine roaring through him.

"Tonight then," Niles agrees.

"Tonight."

17. New Smile

Ruth

We pull up into the grand Demechnef estate driveway at the same time as Niles and Marilynn.

I can hardly keep my eyes open from exhaustion. My clothes are wet and cold with sweat, sticking to my clammy skin like a glove. But as Warrose opens the trunk to pull out my new moving chair, I feel another zing of adrenaline and excitement fire through me.

Niles and Marilynn get to see it! They get to see me move around on my own!

I sit up straight, waiting for him to open my door.

"Hi—that's a new smile," Warrose greets, grinning back at me.

"I want to get in by myself," I tell him eagerly.

He nods, signaling for Niles and Marilynn to come to us. "I'm right here if you need me."

My arms are boneless and feeble as I try to use my upper body strength to grip the arm rests and slide myself from one seat to the other. I groan and whimper as I collapse onto the moving chair.

Warrose leans down, kisses me fiercely on the cheek, then turns me to face my friends.

"What's this?" Niles asks, inspecting the fine details of the carved wood.

"I can move myself around now!" I practically wheeze yet say it all with a wide grin.

"Really?!" Marilynn stands in front of me, looking flushed and a little clammy herself.

"Warrose made it for me!"

It takes a few long seconds for Niles to understand. His beautiful eyes shift from me, to the wheels, to Warrose, then back to me again. He starts to cry in his hand.

A lump instantly wells up in my throat, pushing tears back to the surface when I was so sure I lost them all when I met the Winter Storm Lions.

Marilynn places a hand on his back as his heartbreaking sobs hit us all so hard. It seems the trauma of that prison can slam into us at any time. We can try to mask it, hold it in a dark, untouched place of our minds, but it always comes back in moments that take us by surprise.

And my new chair has taken him by surprise.

Niles kneels down to hug me, gripping a hand on the back of my curly hair, and placing a quick kiss on my forehead. "It's beautiful, Ruthie. Fuck, I'm so happy right now."

"Me too," I tell him.

He stands to face Warrose, holding out his hand to shake. But as Warrose glances down at Niles's hand, they move in for a hug. Niles sobs into Warrose's massive shoulder, saying, "thank you" and "it's a work of art" and "we're going to make it out of that hell one day."

Marilynn traces her hands over the carvings of animals and gargoyles along the trim of my chair. Her full-lipped smile is all-knowing, ancient, and full of a future we have yet to see.

"You know what it looks like?" she asks.

"What's that?"

Her deep, ocean-blue eyes find mine. And they burn like a blaze of forest fire into my soul.

"A throne."

18. The Whip

Ruth

"**I** have so much to tell you about my meeting today," Marilynn gushes as we make our way to the front door.

"Marilynn castrated the Demechnef council!" Niles blurts out.

"*What?*" Warrose and I ask.

I roll my wheels over the threshold to get into the Demechnef estate, breathing in the brisk scent of old books, caramel, and pine. The sconces glitter a rich amber across the dark wallpaper. And that velvet daybed looks too good not to lounge on while I catch up with Niles and Marilynn.

"Well, she *verbally* castrated them!"

"Maybe we could have tea and sandwiches while you tell us all about it," I suggest with a grumbling stomach. After all that hard work earlier, I'm starving.

I catch Warrose's penetrating gaze as I stop in front of the couch. I'm not sure if anyone's ever looked at me like this before. Like he's discovered a hidden mine of pure gold, decorated in rare diamonds. My heart thumps wildly under the weight of those hazel eyes.

He begins to smile at me, but all in the same breath, that smile falls.

Marilynn turns to the stairwell, as if catching on to whatever put a frown on Warrose's face.

"What?" I ask.

Warrose whips his head back to me, holding one finger to my lips.

A creak on the floor sounds to my right, coming from the kitchen and dining room. The moment of silence following it is brief, it's a single breath before something snaps in the air.

I look up to Warrose snatching an arrow mid-air.

His face goes taut, eyes half crest, blind with a quiet rage. With two fingers, he snaps the arrow in half, then seizes a black leather handle from his belt, dragging out his bladed whip. It's heavy and flopping to the glossy floors like a snake, then flashes forward with a loud crack!

"Two on your left, another in the coat closet!" Marilynn shouts.

The whip's precision is without error. The blades slice into flesh, peeling away meat and spurts of blood across the dining room floor. And Warrose doesn't miss a beat. His arm flexes and coils as he aims the handle in a dance of imminent slaughter.

Suddenly Niles is pulling me backward by the handles of my chair, angling our backs against the wall closest to the fireplace.

Another arrow whisks through the air toward Warrose's head. I scream his name without thinking of how my interference could distract him. But thankfully, his whip chops through its dark wood, and ends its path before it lands.

Warrose flicks his wrist to the left once more, beheading a man trying to escape from the coat closet. It falls from bulky shoulders, thumping against the floor in a sickening splash of blood.

"Everyone alright?" he grunts.

We all respond breathlessly, nodding our heads in surprise.

But Warrose is quick to turn to me first, wide eyes scanning over my body in alarm.

"I'm fine, I'm good," I assure him.

He furrows his eyebrows skeptically, then nods once.

Something cold and sharp jabs into my throat along with hot breath curling around my ear. With the knowledge that everyone I know is in eyesight, I scream.

"Don't you fucking move!" Warrose growls, nostrils flaring at the figure behind me, lowered to line up their head with my own so the whip cannot touch him.

"She should have died from that axe!" The thick Old Alkadonian accent is hard to miss. That breath reeks of cigars and meat.

"And you think you're going to live through this? With all your comrades dead and beheaded on my floor?" Marilynn challenges.

"Wait…" Niles says, tense and immovable at my side. "You're the Ringmaster."

"I am not afraid to die if it means saving my country," the Ringmaster says.

My panicked eyes dance around the room before clashing with Warrose's furiously calm stare. I open my mouth to say something to him. Anything. Perhaps something I've been feeling for a long time now. A confession of sorts. One that tells him I never stopped feeling what I was feeling for him in the prison. It never went away. I still look at him and can't breathe.

But my mouth closes.

And no words come out.

The blade lifts from my skin, followed by a victorious yell from the Ringmaster. Before he can jab the tip into my jugular, I turn to my left as a flash of gold snags my attention. Niles grabs the man's wrists and bites down on it. *Hard.*

The Ringmaster roars, standing up from his squatted position behind me.

Warrose jumps at the opportunity Niles has given him. The whip isn't seen, but it is heard. That whooshing sound. Warrose's weapon glides underneath the man's hat. The wet squelch and splatter to the floor. To my right, only the top part of the man's skull and brain roll to the ground.

And Warrose is kneeling in front of me before I've had the chance to blink.

"Did he fucking hurt you?" With careful fingers, he examines my throat as I repeatedly shake my head.

"I'm okay. That was so fast. Niles? Where's Niles?"

"Here." Niles pats my arm, gawking down at the Ringmaster's scalps soaking in a puddle. "I'm here, Ruthie."

"Are you okay?" I ask.

He meets my eyes with a disheveled look. Nods. Tries to smile. Sighs softly.

"I'm sorry it took me that long to act. I was scared."

My sweet Niles.

"I was scared too. Thank you." My heart's racing under my skin, plummeting down my chest. Why were they trying to kill me?

Warrose pinches the bridge of his nose with one hand, caressing my arm with the other.

"I'm safe," I reassure him. "I'm alive because of you."

But opening those hazel eyes to look at me appears to cause him so much physical and emotional pain.

"They're all from Vexamen," Marilynn comments from the dining room, flicking her scarlet red hair over her shoulder. "Maybe soldiers from the breed that wasn't present during the battle when Skylenna got a hold of them?"

"Most likely," Warrose agrees, giving me one last agonized look before he stands, stepping over the bodies to check out the kitchen. Marilynn follows.

They both go eerily quiet.

"Hey!" Niles calls out. We exchange a look.

"Don't come over here," Warrose orders in a flat tone.

Niles and I lock eyes once more. "Pfft!" He nods at me like *of course we have to go over there now.*

I push my wheels forward, despite my exhaustion, despite my aching limp arms. Because something has rendered Marilynn and Warrose speechless. Niles and I move to the other opening of the kitchen, past the body next to the coat closet, and around the corner of the glass cabinets of vintage dining plates.

Turning the corner, Niles and I both come to a staggering stop. At first, we suck in sharp, uncooperative breaths. After that gnawing moment of silence, I let out a disturbed scream.

From the glowing amber chandelier, there hangs a small noose. And from the small noose, hangs a soft white animal. A gaping mouth, gawking eyes, and a tail that swings back and forth.

I wish I could look away from the rest of the kitchen.

I wish to God I could close my eyes. Move any body part at all.

A series of decapitated animal heads of unknown species are lined up along the counter tops, sitting on gooey puddles of bright red blood. And handwritten in blood across the marble floor reads:

Deliésez Ghosëkex Mazonist.

Everyone in the room turns to me with dreadful eyes, waiting.

"Ruth?" Warrose prompts.

I swallow. "It says...*Death to the Mazonist Queen.*"

We take a minute to process that.

"How the hell did they even find out she was a Mazonist?" Niles says.

That's a good question. But then something triggers a memory. "Remember the night of the dinner with the Mazonist Brothers in the prison?" I ask, eyes glazed over as I dissociate from the mess of fur and blood.

"What about it?" Marilynn asks.

"The Mazonist Brothers recognized me. They said I looked like someone."

Everyone looks away to think, to remember that small moment.

"She looks"

"familiar, I know. How very odd. Kind of makes you think"

"But that's absurd. That would mean..." Malcolm trailed off.

I rub my temples. "What if they figured it out? Retraced the footsteps of my lineage? Figure out about the bastard child from the woman Malcolm impregnated?"

"And then they told others," Warrose murmurs huskily, agreeing with my train of thought.

"Yeah. I guess *this* would be the result of that," Marilynn agrees.

Warrose's eyes meet mine, and we don't look away for a long moment. He considers something.

"Marilynn? Have the buggy take you and Ruth back to Skylenna's house."

"Will they be safe there?" Niles asks.

Warrose looks back at the animal parts with a dark, simmering sadness. "It's Skylenna and DaiSzek living there. I can't imagine a safer place on earth."

Marilynn doesn't argue or ask why, she quietly nods and gives me a gloomy smile as we exit the kitchen.

I'm numb and sore as I help myself into the buggy, staring blankly out the window. Those poor animals. I'm heartbroken and nauseated by how that awful country treats their beasts. Who let those traditions happen with the Meat Carnivals? Who could be so vicious? So heartless? What if they had done those terrible things to DaiSzek? To the Winter Storm Lions?

I shudder and swallow down bile as the buggy starts to move.

But as we leave the driveway of Aurick's Estate, I see Chekiss knock on the door.

19. The Package

Skylenna

DaiSzek limps out of the guest bedroom to investigate a potential intruder coming close to our house. He's been healing from a broken leg and ribs after the battle with the Dralutheran. But those wounds don't seem to bother him at all. He still does his perimeter checks, still stands guard at night.

And even though he cannot speak, I can feel his heartbreak echoing through the bond we share. It started with Knightingale's death. That wound has been loud and fearsome, leaving us both with a blistering ache that doesn't ever let up. Through the void, I witnessed the special moments he shared with her.

Oh, how that little girl would follow not far behind when they would scour the woods. How she would tug on his ears like an annoying younger sibling to wake him up in the morning. Any other animal would have hated her. She had the most volatile personality with a wicked temper. But DaiSzek was always patient with her strange nuances. He watched her sleep in the night when it was his turn to guard. He'd endure her small fits of anger when she failed to catch a deer on the run.

She was his special friend that no one else could understand.

And he lost her.

The only moment in his entire life when he was too weak to save the ones he loved.

It broke his heart entirely.

But the real tragedy was that he has been given no time to heal. Not really. His heart wasn't just broken when Dessin fell into that coma.

It was *mutilated.*

There was always a sense of strength and resilience when we all felt Dessin die in that battle. It's like a piece of DaiSzek could sense that this wasn't the end for him.

But now, watching him around Dessin's bed has drained me of all hope. DaiSzek mourns constantly. He whimpers at the foot of his bed, head resting on Dessin's shins. It makes me cry every time I see it. And when I gaze into those cinnamon irises, it's glaringly obvious that DaiSzek is grieving never seeing his best friend again.

It's apparent that Dessin is never coming back.

I've been residing in this guest room with morning sickness all day, curled up in a ball with a thin quilt draped over my body. Lately, it's as if all I can do is hide from the world and wait for my belly to grow in size.

"I want to die," I whisper to the moss-green fabric of the quilt.

A cold breeze seeps through the pinholes of the blanket, chilling my skin with the familiar feeling of death and love tangled within one another.

"It's time to get up now," Scarlett says, her beautiful silhouette kneeling before me on the other side of the quilt.

I throw the covers off of me just as a knock on the door fills the large cottage.

Scarlett disappears.

Opening the oak door, Marilynn is the first face I see.

But my gaze is quickly drawn to the woman seated to her left. Ruby leaves fly across her pretty face, grazing over her upturned, pointed nose.

Ruth blinks up at me.

"What's this?" I ask, pointing to the chair with wheels and grand carvings of animals around its frame.

"Warrose made it for me," she explains, somewhat detached. "It's so I can move around on my own without help."

Something warm and thick gushes into my heart. I hold my chest as I sigh.

"It's beautiful," I utter, admiring the craftsmanship. Admiring her. "You're beautiful."

Ruth almost smiles but doesn't. I kneel on my front porch to hug my best friend, fighting to hold myself together as I use my blanket to keep her warm. *Dessin would be so proud of you, Ruth. He would be so proud of Warrose for making this stunning chair.*

"Can we stay here for a little while?" Marilynn asks.

I pull the quilt around my shoulders as I stand back up. Ruth pats my hand in gratitude.

"Is everything okay?" I ask.

Marilynn shakes her head. "We had somewhat of a hate crime happen at the Demechnef manor."

Adrenaline spikes through my bloodstream. "What kind of hate crime?"

Marilynn glances down at Ruth's blank expression. There's a bleak heaviness in the air. It clots the void with the pungent aroma of death.

"There are members of the Breed still alive. They found out that Ruth is a Mazonist. Let's leave it at that for now." Although her dreamy blue eyes glare into my soul with a silent message. The void nudges me.

I don't have to peer into its vastness for long.

I see the blood.

The animals.

The message.

"Come in." I move to the side, watching in awe as Ruth pushes her wheels over the little bump of the threshold. DaiSzek limps in behind them.

We eat in silence, which is entirely too rare for the three of us. Even in the horrid nature of the prison, there was always something to talk about.

I tear off a piece of bread, watching Ruth move down the hallway. "How is she?" I ask Marilynn.

The gorgeous redhead gulps down soup before meeting my eyes.

"She was doing better before the incident at the estate."

I nod, biting my lip. "What about you and Niles?"

Marilynn sets her bowl down, tracing the rim with her index finger. She looks like she's so close to grinning. Like it's begging, pleading, screaming to come out and show the world how pretty her smile is behind those cherry lips.

"It's going well," she finally murmurs shyly.

I smile. It's not forced, but still feels foreign due to the depression still holding me hostage. "Oh, come on. It's clear you two like each other. What's the hold up?"

A dark overcast blankets that deep ocean blue surrounding her pupils.

"I promised myself for so long I wouldn't get close to any of you," she whispers.

Is that anger lining her tone?

"Because you know how this all ends?" I finish for her.

Tears glaze over her eyes. "Yes and no. It's just…I've hated having my future written for me. I've hated knowing what I know. I made a pact with myself that I wouldn't let my heart get involved."

Definitely anger. It catches fire behind that careful expression.

"But it's Niles…"

"It's Niles," she agrees with a blissfully defeated expression. "He makes my heart sing. How could I ever just ignore that?"

"You can't. He has a heart of gold. It would be a great tragedy to live the rest of your life denying a gift like that." Because it's Niles. He has more loyalty and unfaltering love than most people will ever know. He's *Niles*.

And he deserves true love more than anyone too.

"I'm falling for him whether I try to prevent it or not. It's…inevitable."

I pat her shoulder lovingly and reassure her that what's meant to be, will be. Then I leave the kitchen to find Ruth sitting in Dessin's room, watching him.

"I was telling him about my new chair," she directs to me, though not looking away from his sleeping face.

"Good. He'd be so happy to know that," I say.

"And I was thanking him."

"Oh?"

"For saving me in that prison." Her voice turns hoarse.

And my heart turns brittle.

"For working so hard to keep me from bleeding out."

I lean against the doorframe with a thick, heavy knot forming in my esophagus, making it entirely hard to swallow.

"For making sure I didn't get left behind." Ruth starts to cry.

I bury my face in my hands to try and pull myself together for her. But it's so hard, so terrible, so devastating. He did do all of those things. He would have given up his own happiness, his own life to ensure we all go out alive.

That avenging alter.

Dessin.

"I never got to really thank him when he was awake. I didn't get to tell him how brave he was. How his strength was enough to keep me going. How I had so much faith he wouldn't leave me there."

I sob into my palms but try not to let her hear it.

"I didn't even get to make him uncomfortable with a hug!"

At this, we both laugh through our tears and running noses. Her sharp, narrow shoulders shake as she chuckles, patting the top of his hand fondly.

"He wasn't fond of hugs," I hum in agreement.

But the thing is, he *was* fond of hugs. And not just mine, either. I know for a fact that the last group hug we had in Ruth's cage meant everything to him. The game we played in the stadium, catching each other, having fun despite the terror looming over us…

He loved having a family.

He *loved* hugs.

But while Dessin is lying in that bed, unable to speak, unable to voice his own thoughts and feelingshow can I share such a special piece of him without his consent?

"Why are you standing in the doorway?" Ruth asks, wiping her nose with the back of her hand.

I shrug. "It's hard for me to be in there."

She stares at the back of his hand for a moment, then sighs.

"Every time I lie close to him, I try to find him in the void. I search everywhere." My chest tightens like a twisting screw. "It's going to drive me crazy."

"Have you tried asking for help? I mean from like…those who have passed on?"

I let out a bitter laugh.

"What?"

"I've heard whispers from a few, but they won't show their faces. I don't know if it's because they genuinely don't have answers for me, or because I'm not supposed to have these answers yet."

"What whispers have you heard?" Ruth turns her chair to face me.

"Every now and then, I hear Scarlett encouraging me to keep moving, to get up, to open my eyes, to eat. Then I hear Sophia, Kane's mother, saying one word throughout the night…"

"What word is that?"

I shift my weight on my left leg, gazing out the window to the sharp breeze bustling through the blood-red leaves.

"*Wait.*"

Marilynn opens the front door for DaiSzek, looking down at him as he nudges a box in with his nose. The package slides over the wood floors until it bumps into her feet.

Ruth and I watch her pat DaiSzek on the head from the hallway.

"It's addressed to the three of us!" Marilynn yells.

"Don't open it!" Ruth fusses, rolling toward her. "It could be a trap."

I shake my head. "DaiSzek pushed it through the door. It's safe."

My boy glances up at me with a thoughtful look. He keeps his fractured leg lifted at an angle in the wooden braces Dessin made special for him before…I try not to frown as he hobbles his way over to lay in front of the fireplace.

"Want to read the card?" Marilynn tears off a fringed, old piece of parchment with calligraphy painted over the front.

Ruth nods eagerly.

"It says…"

Ruth, Marilynn, and Skylenna,

You have been formally invited to the Hallows Colony Ball located just beyond the Red Oaks, by the autumn spring.

Inside the box, you shall find the proper garments and attire you'll need to attend.

On this Ancient Hallows night, do not fear if beings of other worlds roam the land, dancing in the darkness…

Tonight is for the ghouls, the drinks, and the magic of the Hallows Colony Ball.

Join us at eight o'clock.

It's been a while since I've seen that look in Ruth's eyes. Those almond irises glitter with intrigue. She begins to smile, and Marilynn and I can't help but grin back.

"DaiSzek, you sure this is safe?" Ruth shouts to him.

He barks once, then drops his head back down to the rug.

"That's a yes." I laugh.

"Should we get ready together?" Ruth is practically vibrating with excitement.

"We should," I say.

"And should I play a record to get in the mood for this creepy ball while also drinking wine?" she adds. "Well, you two can drink juice. I'll have the wine."

"We should do that too."

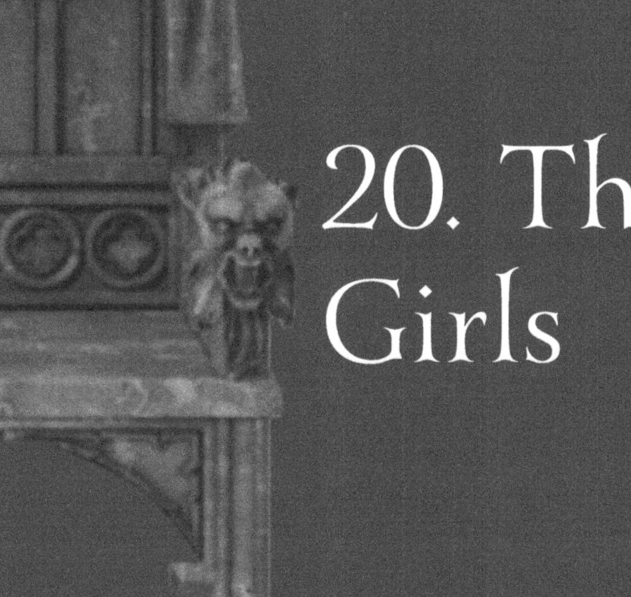

20. The Girls

Marilynn

They aren't your average ball gowns.

They're magical.

One ensemble comes with pointed ears and a glittery opal headdress. Another comes with a tall black crystal and ruby crown, complete with golden curly horns like that of a ram. The last piece has black wispy wings, like that of a dark faerie.

We drink wine and juice, play lovely records to dance to, and help each other put on makeup. The dresses are magnificent, covered in jewels and intricate lacings, buttons, and so long they drag behind us. The package even came with black crystals and red roses to decorate Ruth's chair with.

And as we try on our dresses, I watch the excitement blossom on their faces. My friends. The two women that have endured so much pain, so much agony. Yet they have room in their hearts to smile at something so small.

Why was it so hard to not get attached?

I promised myself I'd keep a distance. That I'd do my duty, but never let my heart get involved. Why was this so terribly impossible?

I thought Niles would be the most difficult to stay away from. The moment I saw him on the day of my return, I lost the breath in my lungs. Yes, I was anxious to see Aurick again. I did love him once. But just looking into those sweet downturned eyes, I lost all of my faculties.

With my time spent in the prison with these women, how could I not fall in love with them too? They're fearsome, resilient, hilarious, brilliant, *loyal*. God, they're so loyal.

"Mar, you look like an elven water nymph!" Ruth claps.

I crack a smile. The flowy dress matches the opal headdress. It looks old and delicate, like from an era of wiccans, curse casters, and magical covens. Skylenna tugs on my pointed earpiece with a grin.

"We ready to go?" she asks.

Skylenna is wearing the shredded black gown with wispy wings and black diamonds lining the breast and midsection bodice. Black lipstick and a smoky cat eye. She's devastatingly beautiful.

Ruth, of course, wears the black crystal and ruby crown with horns, a dazzling ruby gown, and gold jewelry. I finish dusting her freckled cheeks with a scarlet, metallic blush.

I let out a relieved sigh as Ruth admires her face in the mirror, touching her glittered cheekbones with the tips of her delicate fingers.

We take one last gulp of juice, as Ruth finishes her wine, adding final touches to our costumes.

"Ready," I say.

21. Hallows Colony Ball

Ruth

The outdoor ball is held where the red oak trees start to turn burnt orange then gently into yellow. Stepping into a vast opening, we collectively gasp.

Members of the Nightamous Horde are fire dancing, while members of the Stormsage Keep are playing instruments that bring the woodsy area to life.

"Wow," I breathe.

Twinkling globes with small candles, tables of punch bowls, roasted pigs, berries, fruits, copper chalices, autumn wreaths, and a giant campfire fill the space.

Everyone is dressed up. Fae, elves, witches, nymphs, and horned beasts by the dozens.

"Where are the boys?" Skylenna asks.

"I'm going to need to see your invitations," Niles says from behind us.

I roll my chair around to see them standing there, wearing vintage wiccan attire. Niles is wearing brown slacks with a white button-up and suspenders. Warrose is in a manilla linen long sleeve with an open-chest V-neck with ankle-banded bloomers. Chekiss tips his fedora hat to us, dressed in white loose linen and shiny penny loafers.

"Did you boys do all of this?" Marilynn asks.

Niles shrugs. "I mean, I definitely did most of it."

Chekiss rolls his eyes.

"It was Chekiss's idea," Warrose interjects quietly. "We all thought you three could use a fun night out."

His hazel eyes examine the girls next to me, but quickly that gaze flicks back to me, to my gown, to my crown and horns. I try not to look at him, but that stare is crushing.

"How did you arrange it so quickly?" Skylenna eyes Warrose, like she just noticed something that's pulling the corners of her pretty lips upward.

"We had a lot of help from Runa and Asena to set everything up." Chekiss nods to the two women watching us from the punch bowl. "Do you all like it?"

Skylenna answers by giving him a big hug. Marilynn walks into Niles's arms slowly, hesitantly, glancing up at him as if asking for permission to wrap her arms around his waist.

He snorts, tugging her the rest of the way by her shoulders and burying his face into her neck until she starts to laugh.

The feeling of being watched is nearly suffocating. I turn my head to look up at him, catching the way he seems to be waiting on my approval.

"I love it," I announce with a big smile.

The air is sweet, smelling of autumn fragrances. Cinnamon-baked apples, crunchy leaves, and a fresh harvest. I bask in the twinkling lights and fire dancers. I needed this after today.

"You do?" His eyes go round.

"It's so magical. I can't believe you helped do all of this."

He shrugs it off, dropping down to a knee to look up at me. "Want to get a drink?"

"Want to take a shot?" I raise an eyebrow.

The tension in Warrose's shoulders lessens as he lets out a surprised chuckle. The crease between his eyebrows smooths, and he raises his brows back at me.

"Fuck yes, I want to take a shot," he says through another laugh.

I lead the way to the table of drinks and the delicious display of a feast. Passing by the campfire, goose bumps rise on my arms as its warmth radiates through my skin.

I can't believe I'm still able to move this chair despite the aching muscles in my arms. But something about being able to control where I go, how fast I move, and when is liberating, giving me a feeling of bliss in the center of my chest.

"Niles! Take a shot with us?" Warrose calls to the golden boy trying to show Marilynn the new dance he's learned.

"You really want to see a drunk Niles again?" I say under my breath.

Warrose's eyes lose focus as he clearly remembers the Fun House night when we were forced to drink our weight in alcohol and walk a plank. I can't suppress my smile as the memory puts a grumpy look on Warrose's face.

"Oh, damn. That's right," he grunts.

Niles turns around to lock eyes with the big man next to me. He points to the center of his chest in confirmation. "You want to take a shot with *me*?"

As if there's another Niles in the area.

"No, I changed my mind," Warrose replies flatly.

"Of course I would!" Niles does a cute little hop of excitement then rushes over to us.

"That wasn't sarcasm, Niles. I really changed my mind."

Niles tsks at him. "You're funny. Now c'mon! Let's throw a few back!"

"Just one," Warrose grumbles in defeat.

"Five!"

"One."

"Three," I counter.

The boys shoot their eyes to me in surprise.

I shrug. "Or we can just go to bed early and sober."

They chuckle in unison.

"Alright, fine. But you two have to space each shot out. I'll take five," Warrose agrees.

"How is that fair?!" Niles tries to snatch the bottle out of Warrose's bear claw of a fist.

"You are both lightweights."

That's probably accurate.

Niles leans down to my ear, cupping his hands around his mouth. "Don't worry, Ruthie. We'll sneak more when he's not looking! The big ogre is too stupid to see past my tricks."

Warrose hands us our first shot and a small glass with pink juice inside. It's in a funny shape like a miniature pitcher with short red flowers coming out of it.

"Drink it after you take the shot," he instructs.

Niles and I go red in the face as we sneak a fourth shot while Warrose isn't looking.

"I told you," Niles whispers with a slap to his knee. "So stupid."

The autumn costume festival roars with life as people dance, sing, drink, and get warm next to the ferocious campfire. And I haven't felt this good in a long time.

"You're not slick, Niles." Warrose's thick, veiny arm whips around me to snatch the crystal bottle from Niles's drunk grip.

"Were you drinking straight from the bottle?!" I ask in a serious tone, then burst out laughing.

"You're not our baby*sister*!" Niles objects, reaching for the bottle.

"Baby*sitter*," Warrose corrects. A shadowy expression crosses his features. "I guess that role *has* fallen to me."

Niles leans over me to slur, "I'm really not *that* drunk. Honest mistake. Baby *sister*." He laughs to himself.

But Warrose takes a swig of the bottle and walks through the dancing colonial members to the bales of hay in front of the campfire.

"You going to go flirt with Marilynn?" I ask Niles, still watching Warrose's back like a hawk.

Niles glances over his shoulder at the stunning redhead eating a cupcake while also trying to get Skylenna to eat one too.

"I get so serious when I'm around her."

"Why?"

"Nervous." He watches her with suddenly sober eyes. A deep, rich longing.

"Why?" *Do I have any other words in my vocabulary?*

"She has such a heavy presence. Always so retreated in her own head. Always cautious. I get nervous I'll make myself look like a fool," he responds with little slur to his delivery.

I want to make a joke that he *always* makes himself look like a fool, but something about the way he looks across the festival at her shimmering ruby hair makes me pause.

"She likes you, Niles." I set my glass down, feeling warmth and endorphins swim in my chest.

"You think?"

"Pluck up the courage and go ask her to dance," I order.

"Twist my arm why don't you!" And he's off, speed-walking in the direction of Marilynn and the dessert table.

Marilynn

The way Skylenna watches couples dance, drink, and kiss among the harvest leaves and fire breaks my heart. I don't think I've ever felt more guilt in my entire life.

As those emerald orbs scan the crowd of people, a heavy rope of longing wraps around her body, tightening each muscle.

"I wish he was here too," I say quietly.

Skylenna stiffens and glances at me from the corner of her eye. She offers a sad smile.

"He snuck into a ball once when he was an asylum patient…just to share a dance with me." Her glowing eyes are lost somewhere in a memory.

"Hard to imagine him making grand romantic gestures." I force a laugh.

"And to tell Aurick if he ever hit me again—Dessin would make him watch while he castrated him," she adds.

We both laugh.

Skylenna releases a deeply painful sigh. "You know so much about his future that you can't say, can you?"

The guilt strikes through my heart again like a vengeful bolt of lightning.

I keep my gaze far away from her.

She nods in defeat, dabbing a tear away from her black makeup.

Her sniffle is blended with a laugh. "I'm crying all the time now. I know the hormones are brutal, but this is exhausting."

My chest bleeds, twisting and clenching down in pain. I'm going to hell, aren't I?

"Skylenna—"

"Don't." She holds a shaky hand up. "I know you can't tell me anything."

"We took an oath. We…"

But her face rests as if she's already passed away. There's no life there anymore. No hope. No reason to keep going.

I remember the day I had to take the oath with Judas. We did it every year with the gathering of our people in the Red Oaks. The instinct to protect all information in the prophecy has literally been burned into our brains since birth. Every. Single. Year.

But her face…

"You won't find relief any time soon," I finally blurt out.

Skylenna turns to me with her hands wrapped around her torso, holding herself in defense of the pain she feels.

"But you will. Dessin's story is far from over." *God is going to stop my heart right here, isn't he?*

"What?" She places that frail, tan hand over her lips.

"Just…take good care of your pregnancy, okay? Take good care of those babies."

I know I've royally fucked myself when I watch her mouth fall open at my minor slip up.

"Babies? Plural? Am I having twins, Marilynn?" she cries, voice muffled into her hand.

"Damn," I say, hanging my head.

"Twins." Her eyes flood with tears, both happy and melancholy. "Kane and I were both twins."

I give her a close-lipped smile and nod.

"Oh my god!" she squeals in delight, throwing her arms around me.

Hugging her weak body to my chest. "You'll never know what this has done for me. Thank you! Thank you!"

And how can I regret my decision to give her the slightest bit of hope? Look how happy she is. Who am I to keep this news from her?

"Okay, yes, I'm nervous around you. But I'm here anyway to ask you to dance!" Niles appears in front of us, throwing his hands in the air dramatically.

Skylenna snickers, wiping her eyes quickly.

"Oops…did I interrupt a moment?"

"No!" Skylenna laughs wetly. "Please, dance with her! She deserves it!"

I raise my eyebrows at her, but she simply nods with encouragement, giving me a shove in his direction. *"Thank you,"* she mouths.

Niles guides me to the center of the dancing crowd, then turns to bow.

"I really can't stop staring at you. It's an illness."

I smile, taking his hand, and letting him pull me into his warm body. I let the side of my head rest against his jaw, and he breathes me in, ruffling the hairs on my head with his nose.

I imagine growing old with him, dancing slowly like this to our favorite string quartets.

"About earlier…" he prompts.

"Yes?"

Niles hesitates. "Did I cross a line?"

I grin against his shoulder. "No. I've been wanting that to happen too."

The memory of his fingers tracing my panties sends a thrill up my spine, and I arch against him. Deep breaths.

"Hmm," he hums in thought. Those soft lips graze my temple. "I can't stop thinking about it."

My stomach flutters as his lips continue to explore my skin, my hair, placing gentle kisses in a trail that sets me ablaze.

Fuck. Now that the morning sickness has subsided, touching Niles is absorbing my every thought. I want to tell him how I really feel. I'm fighting the demons in my mind that are telling me to keep my distance, protect myself from this prophecy. Leave and never come back.

"Are you wet again?" he asks, low in my ear.

So much so that my inner thighs are slick as we dance. "Yes."

He groans. "How am I supposed to think clearly the rest of the night?"

Our bodies melt into each other, savoring the burning sensation of pleasure we're experiencing simultaneously. Our breath and heartbeats stringing together, conjuring an animal-like frenzy as we dance.

But to bring everything to a halting stop, my stomach grumbles.

Niles laughs. "Baby comes first, yes? Let's raid the feast?"

"Please." My cheeks stain in embarrassment.

We leave the dance, sit by the long table of colorful foods and drinks, and I eat while Niles rubs my calves.

"You like taking care of me," I comment.

Niles smiles, continuing to knead into my muscles.

"It's turning me on," I add.

His hands pause. Eyes flash up to meet mine. There's a steady stream of thoughts that take root in his mind, furrowing that smooth brow for a moment.

"As if I need more motivation to keep touching you." He shakes his head, focusing on my leg again. "Will you—stay with me tonight?"

My entire body softens. I run a hand through his soft, golden hair, savoring the silky texture against my fingertips. Niles lets his eyes fall shut at my caress.

"I will."

Ruth

I waste no time, straining my arms to get my chair from the table of drinks to the campfire. Nerves jet through my fingertips at the sight of his broad, bulky back.

"Are you going to ask me to dance or not, chicken coward?"

He lifts his chin and narrows his eyes. "I'd love to dance with you, little rebel."

"Good. Is this chair big enough to support your huge ass?" I deadpan.

Warrose throws his head back to laugh. "I did have to test its durability with this huge ass. Why?"

My chest flutters and spins from the sound of that gravelly, baritone laugh.

"And are those arms strong enough to push us around?" I add.

Warrose's sultry eyes twinkle as he picks apart my idea in his head. "They should be."

"Do you think you could sit in my chair, and set me in your lap so you can twirl us around to the next song?"

His jaw flexes as he goes quiet for three seconds. He nods twice, rising from his seat.

"Put your arms around my neck," the beautiful, burly man instructs.

Chills climb up my arms, burrowing into each cell of my skin.

I do as he requests, hugging myself to that thick neck, breathing in his smoky, spiced scent that sends waves of happiness to my core.

"You smell so good," I comment. My eyes go wide. *Whoops.*

"You smelling me, little rebel?"

"Absolutely not."

Oh, but I am. His clothes smell clean. But his skin always has this rich scent of the outdoors, burning wood, and something sweet.

His chuckle is lush and rumbling.

"Down you go." He lowers me to his lap now in the chair gently. "You smell good too."

A zap of excitement jolts through me. My slightly drunk brain doesn't know how not to gawk at him with my satisfaction. How not to keep taking deep, happy inhales to continue filling my mind with that rustic, saccharine scent around him.

With one arm around his neck and the other in my lap, I hold on as he rolls us out closer to the source of the whimsical music. Violins. Harps. Other string instruments I don't recognize.

He spins and twirls us in my chair, careful not to hit anyone else dancing. I form a happy sigh, then say, "You know what would make this better?"

"What's that?"

"For you to hum to the music."

He chuckles before obliging me. The low rumbling of his chest nearly brings tears to my eyes. It's gruff and soothing, entwining with the musical notes around us like milk and honey spooling together. I release another happy little sigh and rest my head against his neck as he continues to move us with the beautiful sounds in the air.

And maybe it's the alcohol, maybe it's the magic in this forest, maybe the fairytale picturesque ball in the autumn weather…but with my right hand, I play with his hair, running my fingers into his silky, thick locks. And with the other hand, I caress his chest through his open shirt, grazing my fingers along the dark dusting of chest hair.

Those massive pectoral muscles turn to stone, bulging under my fingers. He sits up straighter with breaths that are uncooperative with an uneven rhythm.

"Your skin is so soft," he sighs, eyes fluttering close, showcasing a fan of black lashes that grazes the skin under his eyes.

"We're dancing," I hum.

Warrose's softened face tightens up again with a slow creeping smile. He spins us a little faster to the music hitting a faster rhythm. I squeal at the whirling lights and glittering gowns that pass me in the rotation of my moving chair. He laughs out loud, grinning now.

"Faster!" I point my finger forward like we're riding into battle. "Onward!"

He tosses his head back to laugh harder as he charges my wheels in opposite directions. I arch my back and take in the breeze drifting through my hair and crown, screaming as the music bursts to life, as if the musicians have been inspired by our wild dancing.

A quick kiss to my arm, followed by more chuckling. It shifts my delirious, happy mind for a split second. Did he just kiss my arm? The one wrapped around his neck? Why would he do that? What does it mean?

"Do you?" I shout to him over the blaring music, forgetting he isn't an audience member to my spiraling thoughts.

He's still grinning. "Do I what?"

"The prison!"

Warrose laughs, throaty and confused. "Complete your sentences, little rebel!"

"You had feelings for me in the prison!" *Welp, guess there's no going back now.*

Anticipation curls its talons in my chest, clenching around my heart. Am I too bold? Am I too drunk?

His expression loses its warmth as his smile starts to fall. The understanding of my question is blatant as I watch the thoughts process behind his glimmering hazel gaze.

"I know I'm not who I was when you kissed me then!" I start to back over my own words, panting in his face. "I'm not the same Ruth you spent time with. I know that! I've lost a lot of color to my skin. My hair has been coming out. My eyes look sick all the time. And I can never get warm. I know, I know!"

Are my cheeks wet?

"But maybe in time I can be what you like again. Maybe I can be what you want! Maybe"

"Do you still want me, Ruth?" Warrose has never looked so serious.

The chair slows down, but we don't stop moving.

I nod as a tear falls to his lap. "I do still want you."

He loses his breath as it flushes out of his lungs. That broad upper body nearly deflates before my eyes.

"Thank fucking God," he says in a raspy, strained voice.

The chair stops abruptly. The music soars to life again. A burst of tawny fireworks explodes overhead. Those bronze, giant hands swallow the sides of my face.

And Warrose presses his lips to mine in a fevered exhale.

I practically sob in relief as I instantly recognize the taste of his mouth, the rough sensation of his facial hair against my chin. His kiss isn't gentle and patient like last time in my cage. He supports the back of my head, holding me close to his face as he tastes my lips urgently. I part my mouth for him with a tipsy moan, sliding my hands up the bulk of his chest.

With his forehead pressing against my own, he kisses me like he's been waiting for me to come home to him. From that prison. From that stage. He's been waiting for *me*.

How did I not notice before? That large erection pressing against my center. Pleasure thrums through me, leaving my inner thighs slick and wet.

His hot breath skims my tongue as he groans my name, saying over and over again, "Thank God."

I want to tell him now. The feelings I have are burrowed deep in my chest. It's more than attraction. It's far stronger, far more durable. It's enough to bring me out of the darkness, mute my pain even if it's only for a little while. I'm going to tell him…

"This looks like the start of an orgy party!"

The music slows to a stop at that hauntingly familiar voice.

A crowd parts as Skylenna takes a few steps forward to see the source of the voice approaching from the shadows of the heavy overhang of flaming yellow leaves.

Two large women. Furs and cloaks. Giant swords strapped to their backs.

Women of the East Vexello Mountains.

22. "For where you go, I will go."

Ruth

"Helga Bee!" Skylenna rushes to our brave friends with open arms. "Gerta!"

"Greetings to our small friends in the north!" Helga Bee does a little fist pump.

"I'm so glad you made it home okay," Skylenna says.

"We wouldn't leave until the prisoners were freed," Helga Bee smiles proudly, patting Skylenna on the back.

A chill spreads over my cheeks. Warrose's hands have let me go, shifting away slowly. I spin back to face him, finding him watching me with a furrowed brow and thoughtful, brooding eyes.

I should say something.

But he acts quicker than my thoughts turn to actions. With a swift shift of his weight, he lifts me off his lap and sets me down on my chair. I don't miss the way he readjusts his pants.

Niles and Marilynn join us as we greet Helga Bee and Gerta.

"*Perty* boy," Gerta gushes, running a stumpy finger along his shoulder.

"Yes, I know, Niles very perty." Niles gives the top of her head a quick pat.

"Have you come to live here?" Skylenna asks them.

Helga Bee slaps her on the back with an obnoxiously loud chuckle. "We're mountain folk! Why would we ever come to this dump? No offense, little lady."

Skylenna raises her eyebrows at us with a smile that says *some things haven't changed.*

"Why are you here?" Warrose asks.

Helga Bee and Gerta flash their gazes down to me, a quiet nod of acknowledgment. They exchange a knowing look, then meet my eyes again.

"Our country's been thrown into chaos since the war. The Meat Carnivals are louder and scarier than ever, even though the animals were released. Groundskeepers managed to get most of them back. There are still members of the Breed lingering about to make things worse."

"But the Mazonist Brothers are gone. Shouldn't that be a step up from how things were before?" Warrose places a protective hand on my shoulder.

"No leader*thip*. No order," Gerta replies with a lisp.

"People are waiting," Helga Bee adds.

"For what?" Skylenna runs the back of her fingers over DaiSzek as he limps forward.

The mountain women glance down at me again. "For the last living Mazonist heir to make our country a better place."

All eyes fall back to me.

"Your people aren't the only ones who were given a prophecy."
Wait... What?

Skylenna turns to me with speculative eyes, then finds Asena and Runa in the crowd of members from the different colonies here. They don't nod or confirm what's being said. They merely watch her, waiting to see how she fits this all together in her head.

"Vexamen received a prophecy about us too?" Skylenna mutters. She looks to her left as if wanting to share a conspiratorial look with someone who will understand where her thought process has taken her.

But he isn't there.

And the collapse of her expression says it all. The last leaf falling in a winter breeze. Hope perishing before my very eyes.

"Gerta and I were caught on purpose, blondie. We knew your family would one day need allies in that place. Subtle, but we were there in the shadows watching history unfold just the same." Helga Bee crosses her thick arms proudly. "But more importantly, we came to get to know the heir. To see if she was worth laying down our lives for in battle. To see if she has the right kind of heart to rule a catastrophic nation."

They're all looking at me.

I don't know what to do with my hands.

"And what kind of heart does she have?" Warrose asks, holding on to my shoulder without a lapse in pressure.

Helga Bee moves through my friends to get to me. "We saw you give a piece of your soul that day on the execution block. We saw you sacrifice for your people."

A lump forms in my throat. Flashbacks of the axe scrape across my vision in a burst of scarlet floods and hysterical screams. Warrose's teary bloodshot gaze. Dessin covered in my blood. Skylenna holding my head in her lap. *The pain. The pain. The pain.*

"Your whole life people must have mistaken you for a lamb, huh?" she says, resting her hands on her knees to get a better look at me. "But you're a lion in there. Still sleeping."

Pressure builds like a dam behind my eyes. She's calling me strong. She's calling me a…*leader.*

Helga Bee looks up at Warrose, as if forgetting to answer his question. "She's got the heart of a lion."

I release something mixed between a sob and an exhale. "Are you asking me to run your country?"

That must be a mistake…

Gerta arrives behind Helga Bee, dropping down to a knee with her. "Yes."

"I would never be accepted. I'd never be able to influence anyone. Look at me!"

Doubt. Shame. Horror.

Their faces remain patient and forgiving. "Your reign is written in the halls of our mountain temples, dear queen. It is inevitable. All the good you'll do. All the lives you'll save."

But I can't stop shaking my head. Can't stop crying in silence.

"For the one that bled from the blade will sit in her kingdom, in the only throne to move from land to sea. For the one that bled from the blade will break the chains of man and beast. The only army to run on all fours. For the one that bled from the blade will rule until old and gray," Helga Bee and Gerta recite from heart.

The mountain women unsheathe their swords, placing them over their chests as they bow.

"For where she goes, we will go. For where she fights, we will be her sword."

Helga Bee glances up at me. *"Long live the last Mazonist."*

I place a clammy hand on her shoulder, surprised I'm not embarrassed by all the attention this is bringing me. My old friends from the prison are remarkably genuine and determined to have my back. To watch me succeed.

"There are so many there who want me dead. They've already threatened me here," I whisper to her. "I'm not Skylenna. I'm no good to anyone in a fight over a throne I didn't even know I could have possibly inherited. You'd be putting misguided faith into someone who can't protect your people."

Helga Bee glances at my quivering hand, then smirks. "Why don't you ask him? The one who redirects the whip from beast to man?"

I raise my brows at Warrose to see if he is understanding what she's saying, because I'm not. Nope, in fact, my slightly buzzed brain is only working on new routes to let these pure souls down easily.

"I…I have always planned on traveling to Vexamen to stop the Meat Carnivals. I wondered that if I freed them, where would their allegiance then lie?" Warrose meets my eyes, keeping a watchful eye on me as we both try to put together what they're saying.

"Think on it, folks. Our boat leaves tomorrow at sunset. We'll wait for you on the southern shore!"

"You want her to leave with you?!" Skylenna gasps.

Helga Bee nudges Gerta with an elbow. "Did she just now get to the party or what?"

"You want her to go back to that cursed hell that we worked so hard to save her from?" Skylenna reiterates her question with a venomous bite to her words.

...we worked so hard to save her.

Save her.

I know what she means. I understand the intent. There wasn't a scenario where I survived in that prison if left there any longer. Yet the way Skylenna's stepping forward with clenched fists and a defensive stance is making me feel so small, so helpless.

So weak.

And strength? Most wouldn't have survived what you have endured. You are far stronger now than you were when we entered that godforsaken place. You're a born leader who now knows great suffering and deep-rooted grief.

I lift my chin in quiet protest. "I'll think about it."

Warrose's hand goes still on my shoulder.

"No," Skylenna mutters as she spins around to face me. "You can't go back. Not after everything. Not while you're still healing!"

"Don't make me feel weak, Skylenna." I hold up my hand to stop her. "Don't do that. I am not weak. I. Don't. Like. It."

She closes her mouth as she's taken aback, scanning my expression with sudden surprise that glows bright in her glistening emerald eyes.

Niles places a hand on her back. "She's right, Skylenna. Ruth's got the heart of a lion. She can do whatever she puts her mind to."

But my friend just stares at me, unmoving, unblinking, unwilling to lower her guard and relax the tension wrinkling her brow. Instead, she walks away. Her long wispy black dress trailing over the scorched leaves in her wake.

I turn to Helga Bee and say again, "I'll think about it."

23. "I've waited so long."

Marilynn

When I was eleven, I tried to run away to Alkadonia. Judas caught me climbing out the window, dangling from the second story like a ragdoll. I remember how stunned he was to find out I wanted nothing to do with this prophecy. He stared at my fingers clamped around the window ledge, rubbing the back of his neck as he shook his head.

"Aren't you excited to meet all of them? You're so lucky, Lynn. You have a far greater role to play in this than I do." He huffed and helped me climb back into my room. "What about your son? If you leave now, that boy won't go down in history. He's going to go places no one has ever—"

"You really can't figure out why I'd want to get as far away from that future as I can possibly get? *Really?* Not an inkling?!" I cried, throwing my bag to the floor.

Judas hung his head.

And even though I stayed, that was the last we'd ever speak about my part to play in this prophecy.

Watching Niles carry my bags into the quiet inn just outside of the city breeds anger deep in my belly. He did all of this without needing to be told. The initiative is effortless. A silent stream that flows through his being without a beginning or end.

"Now, I know you've been craving dark chocolate and roasted pecans lately, so I brought a bag just for that. We could feed a small village with it," Niles says, bumping open the inn door with his hip to reveal a small room, a cast iron chiminea fireplace, a queen-size feather bed with the thickest blankets and fluffiest white pillows.

After the festival, we didn't want to go back to the Demechnef manor. Especially after it was broken into. The ball seemed to dwindle down after our mountain friends departed, and Ruth had a lot to consider. I decided it was best that I leave early to avoid talking about it with them, considering I already know what her choice will be.

"Do your feet still ache?" Niles sets the bags down. "I brought that lavender oil so I can massage them tonight."

My gut spins into an aching spiral of grief. *I. Don't. Want. To. Love. Him.* And how could I ever imagine it wasn't going to be this hard? He's a phenomenal man of the highest respect. Niles Offborth has the sweetest, purest soul of anyone in this world.

I don't deserve him.

I've spent the better part of my life trying to hate him so I wouldn't adore him or fantasize about the day I might meet him. And here he is, laying out my favorite snacks, prepping to rub my sore feet in front of the black cast iron fireplace.

I feel absolutely powerless to prophecy.

"My feet do hurt," I say in a hushed tone.

He glances up at me with those gorgeous doe eyes. "Here, I put pillows down. Get warm by the fire, and I'll take care of you."

I'll take care of you.

My heart clenches.

"Okay." I drop down to the large pillows he angled to support my bottom and back.

And Niles does just that. He takes care of me, offering pieces of dark chocolate for me to eat while lathering his hands in oil and kneading the heel of my foot.

I let my head fall back with an elated sigh.

So good.

His strong fingers are methodical with their movements to relieve the ache. The sensations fill me with an unrelenting desire that stems from earlier today.

"Are you still drunk?" I ask.

He laughs. "No."

"Not at all?"

"Not since you were making me taste-test all *ninety-seven* dishes with you at the ball."

I snicker.

"There's a smile!" He points with a grin. "You've been scowling ever since we left the party."

"No, I have not."

"Yes, you have. But it's okay. You have the cutest pouting lips I've ever seen."

I tuck my bottom lip into my mouth self-consciously.

"You had me worried there for a minute. I thought you were mad at me," he adds.

"Mad? No. Why would you think that?" I say.

Niles shrugs. "Everyone is always mad at me."

I laugh. I guess that's kind of true.

His smile is radiant as he watches the aftereffects of my laugh fade across my mouth like a dissolving ocean wave.

"I was worried you were regretting…earlier today with me," he finally declares more seriously. Niles scoops his fingers into a glass jar of body cream, massaging into my toes until I'm turning soft and gushy before his eyes.

"No," I moan. *Shit, that feels so good.* "I don't regret it."

He pauses his thumbs for a moment as he recalls something. Beguiling turquoise eyes losing focus as they veer to the left.

"You rubbed my feet every night in that prison," he states.

My heart fills with a longing so intense, I can swear it's bleeding into my soul.

"You stayed up with me because I was too scared to fall back asleep from the nightmares of the fire."

I nod once.

His eyes glisten.

"Can I tell you a secret, Marilynn?"

"Always."

He pulls in a sharp breath. Continues to massage my heels.

"I was being experimented on by Mind Phantoms before I was committed to the insane asylum. I didn't know it then. But they made me do horrible things to people. *Good* people."

I watch him without an ounce of judgment crossing my expression. My brother, Judas, has always told me how annoyingly judgmental I've been my entire life. I've had very little patience, very little tolerance.

But not tonight. Not for him.

"I remember wandering around aimlessly through the Bear Traps, depressed, confused, and delirious on a cool spring day. I saw a man and woman arguing by a stream. Not just arguing. They were at each other's throats. He shoved her into the stream and said something unforgivable about her father, I think. She began to sob right there in the mess of wildflowers and muddy water pooling around her."

Oh, God. I know where this is going. I've just never heard it from the source.

"I intervened. Deescalated the fight. Offered them a meal and—drugged their food."

I don't let the surprise cross my face as he inspects my reaction.

"I was convinced I could spot a pair of soul mates. That I was somehow special. I thought I could sense that their souls were destined to be together, and that if I put them in a hostile environment where they were forced to bond, then perhaps they would realize their love for each other. Perhaps I could prove true love exists. That I was in fact…special."

My heart wilts around the edges. He stays quiet for another minute.

"Go on. I'm listening," I say.

"I held them captive, Mar. Locked them in my basement. Made the man think I was torturing and killing the woman. And I mean, my plan worked a little. He got territorial over her. Extremely protective. The strange thing is, he eventually broke free, and I was certain he was going to kill me." Niles pauses his fingers over my ankles. "He said something I'll never forget. He held a dagger to my throat, looked me in the eye, and said, '*Now you get to live the rest of your life knowing you weren't as strong as Charles. Don't ever forget my words. Because I'll never forget what you've done here.*'"

I can hardly breathe. "How could he know about your father?"

Niles stares off in a daze.

"I honestly don't know. Those words have haunted me for a very long time."

An icy chill is sprinkled over my back and legs. This is one area I'll never be able to relate to him with. Niles has known suffering since he was a little boy. He has seen too much, too young. And I'll never be able to fully understand how those horrible events have altered his mind and way of thinking.

"I saw something in his eyes that day when he untied her from the bedposts." Niles winces at those last two words.

"What did you see?"

"Love," he says in an exhale. "Not that he was willing to admit it. But it was there."

I sigh as he massages up my right calf.

"I was scared I'd never get to look at someone that way. I was scared I'd die without love. Without a woman to hold." Those sparkling round eyes find mine, and they stay there. "You protected me in that prison. You fought for us in that war. You held my hand through those bars and never said a word to anyone about how scared I was…"

His voice quivers, and he tugs me by my legs across the floor so that he's leaning in my face.

"You called me your hero and made me love you in that cold, dark cage."

I completely lose my breath, shuddering at his confession.

"You…you *what*?!"

He flashes me that special Niles smile. "You've made me *love* you, Marilynn, sweetheart. You've given me a woman to hold and a soul to match my own…if you'll have me. I know I'm not a protector like Warrose or Dessin. I'm not stoic or skillful. You can probably protect me a hell of a lot better than I can protect you."

I watch him take my soft hands and hold them to his chest earnestly.

"But I have so much love in my heart to give you. I have so much love in my heart to give your baby. I promise to worship you day and night, to give you more affection than you could ever want for. I…have so much love for you, Mar. Will you have me?"

"*Yes*," I choke out. "Oh, Niles. Yes. *Yes*. I'll have you. I've loved you for so long."

My chest bursts with bottled emotions as he swallows me in his embrace, tugging once more to have me scooped into his lap. And he can't help but advance on me, inhaling my lips before he gives me a quick, gentle kiss. Then another. And another. Though, a lust too infectious comes over him, and he flicks his tongue out to taste my bottom lip.

As I release a sweet, quiet moan, Niles places his thumb on my chin to open my mouth a little more. He licks the inside of my mouth and lets his eyes fall shut, savoring the taste.

My dress is hiked up, revealing my thighs, nearly exposing my panties. His palms clutch the round underside of my ass, pulling me tight until I'm flush against his long erection. A mewl escapes me as I roll my hips and tease my clit against his length.

"I've thought about this so many times in the prison," Niles admits.

"But you didn't try anything at the Ecstasy Night," I pant against his face.

I rock against him, and fire blazes in his orbs.

"I was being a gentleman," he grumbles, digging his fingers against my ass.

"You could have been a gentleman who was licking my pussy."

The veins in his neck protrude as he meets my eyes with half-crest lids and genuine surprise parting his lips. "Christ, Marilynn."

Slipping his hands under my dress, he plays with the lining of my cotton panties, manipulating my hips to dry fuck him in a slow lazy motion. We both suck in a pained breath before a loud moan rips from my throat.

"Niles," I gasp, tensing as my panties soak through to his pants. "More. Please."

After a few more times forcing my hips to roll against him, we hear a wet slurping sound coming from my pussy rubbing up against him. He pauses my hips, looking down with hazy eyes at the shiny spot on his pants.

"Whoops," I mutter.

"How wet are you?"

I look down again at the gushing mess I'm making between us.

"I'm sorry," I burst, scrambling to put some distance between us so I can clean some of it up. *Why the hell am I this wet?*

"*Sorry?!*" Niles flips me onto my back carefully, hiking up my dress to get a better look. "Sweetheart, you're soaking for me."

I blink up at him, legs spread so he can examine my drenched panties.

"I…I don't think I've ever been harder in my entire life," he adds.

"Really?" I shiver as he caresses my soft inner thighs.

"My mouth is watering, I mean…" He acts on instinct and leans down between my legs, inhaling deeply. His eyes roll back into his head.

I sigh at the sight of him kneeling for me, bowing between my thighs.

"So wet." He drags two fingers down the center of my underwear and holds his hand out for me. Clear arousal stretches between his index and thumb. I'm embarrassingly wet.

"*Jeeze,*" is all I can muster.

"I want to make love to you now, sweetheart, I do. But I can't leave you like this. I need to clean you up. I mean, I have to, right?"

I begin nodding with more embarrassment staining my cheeks. *Damnit, Marilynn. What the actual hell. You're grossing him out on the first night together.*

Niles is in a daze as he slips my panties down my legs, yanking them off my ankles in a hurry. I freeze as he starts to lick my juices from the center of that cotton fabric.

"What—what are you doing?!"

Niles groans, breathing in through his nose to capture the scent again.

Does he—like it?!

"I'm addicted. You smell so good." His eyes drop to my spread legs, mesmerized with my pussy now exposed for him.

"I've made a mess," I say in a trance.

Niles drops my panties and crawls to me, turquoise eyes fixated on my warm center.

"I may not even get the chance to make love to you tonight, love." He pushes my thighs apart an inch further as he stares at my opening. "I don't know if I'll be able to move on from licking you. And fuck, look at your round belly." He hikes my dress up further to caress my small baby bump. It's all turning him on. My pregnancy. All of me.

"*Oh,*" I sigh, feeling myself flutter open, lubricating my entrance even more now.

"You just keep pulsating. I can see you getting wetter at the sound of my voice."

It's true. My lower belly is flooding with heat as he talks sweet and soft, breathing me in while he's lying on the ground to get a better look at me.

"Can I eat you now, Mar?" His lips tickle mine.

My mouth is dry. I can hardly get that one damn word out. "Yes."

Niles kisses my clit once, groans, kisses it again. I shudder at the agonizing rush of endorphins pouring into my bloodstream.

"So soft," he hums to himself.

His tongue runs up one of my lips, then again on the other one. Judging by the way he explores me, it's clear he knows his way around a woman's body.

"Oh!" I gasp, clutching my hands around air as he tastes my clit. It buzzes with scorching heat. I can hardly contain my reaction. Squirming. Bucking. Clenching around air.

"Is that sensitive?" he murmurs, dabbing the pad of his index finger over my light pink skin.

I buck again.

"Mmm." He nods, stroking my center gently. "*Gushing.*"

My ass slides on the hardwood floor. Oh god, I really am making a mess.

"I'mit's all over the floor. You'rekilling me."

Niles drops his eyes to the floor, grumbling softly. Without waiting any longer, he does exactly what he said he would do. He laps me up, languidly running his tongue over the wettest parts of me. I'm blinded by the slurping sensations happening between my lips.

"Niles!" I cry, hooking my hands in those soft golden locks.

That tongue dips into my hole, making a delicious effort to taste me on the inside. Like my wetness just isn't enough to satisfy his sweet tooth for me. He needs more.

More. More. *More*.

My back arches upward. He's massaging my ass. Fingers curling into my skin. A crazed state of licking and sucking my swollen clit.

I'm a pit of fire. A well of moans, gasps, writhing euphoria.

How have I gone so long without him?

How did I not beg for his touch in the prison?

"Your scent—burns in my memory now," he says, muffled against my sensitive cunt.

And with a light clucking of his tongue, he sucks on my clit. A ravenous pull that lights up my bundle of nerves, causing my hips to buck against his mouth without warning.

Niles hums in a delirious state, vibrating my clit. The pleasure is a cord I can no longer hold close. It stretches tighter, then breaks free. A downpour of liquid rushing through my lower body that's both ice cold and scorching hot.

My back bows as every muscle bears down.

"Tastes so sweet," Niles comments as he devours my orgasm. "*More*."

"No!" I nearly shout. My clit is a live wire of sensitivity. "Please! Ticklish."

To my surprise, he laughs against me. The soft, funny sound makes me grin like a fool.

"I want to keep eating," he responds.

I prop myself up on my elbows, struggling to fight past the boneless feeling in my limbs.

"I've been waiting half my life for you, Niles. Please, make love to me. You have the rest of your life to eat me every day."

I want to cry as sudden realization flickers across his golden face. "I can keep you."

Tears well in my eyes. "You can keep me."

I lie back for him, peeling off my dress so that he may see all of me. My large breasts drop out from my brassiere at the same time his long cock springs from his pants. It's so hard, the sensation must be aching for him.

Niles climbs over me, trapping me in his arms and natural body heat. I can't think of a sweeter place in the whole world. His lips fuse with mine, and he positions his hips to line up the tip of his cock with my wet opening.

He kisses me all over, letting the head of his dick rest in my fluttering opening. I'm mewling and grinding, desperate to finally have him.

Niles pauses over my swollen, tender breasts, gazing down at them as he circles his thumbs over my hard nipples.

"When will you start lactating?"

I pause. "What?"

There's a drunk glint in his eyes. "You heard me."

"I don't know…when I give birth? Why?" I can't help but smile up at him.

"You have gorgeous breasts, Mar." His eyes trail over them with subtle obsession. "Drinking from you would drive me fucking crazy. They're so perfect."

My body flushes with scorching heat. "You—want to taste my breast milk?"

A delirious, crazed animal stirs inside of me.

"Yes," he says with hooded eyes. "Like this." Niles bends down to capture my left nipple in his mouth, sucking gently, then taking more of my breast into his mouth to get more of me. He groans and uses the head of his cock to add pressure to my opening.

He lifts his head. "Say it to me again, my beautiful Marilynn."

"Say what?"

I can't think. Can't breathe. I want him so badly.

"What you said to me in the prison," he rasps against my ear.

I force myself to see past the murky clouds of my lingering orgasm. What did I say to him? What could he mean? Oh…

"You're my hero, Niles."

He moans against the side of my face, jolting his hips forward, slamming himself all the way inside me.

I hiss at the impact, clawing helplessly at his back.

"I don't know what's gotten into me," he murmurs, pumping into harder this time. "I want to take my time."

"But what?" My pants of pleasure echo against the walls.

"But I'm going to make love to you like a madman. Is that okay?"

"Have me anyway you want, baby," I choke out. "You'll make love to me many times after this. We have time."

"We have time," he repeats as if in a hypnotic state.

My heart could explode right now. Right here.

His hips undulate, and I follow his rhythm. He presses his face against my breasts, leaving delicate kisses until he's sucking on my nipple.

"I'm going to come if I say what I want to say right now." He buries his face between my breasts in defeat, pushing their weight against his cheeks.

My interest is sparked. "Say it."

"No…" He shakes his head.

"Please say it. I'm desperate to feel you come."

Niles sighs, looking up at me as if he's drowning in emotions.

"You're my soulmate," he stammers, slamming into me again. "I'm going to love you for the rest of my life."

And as he latches onto me, pushing his orgasm inside of me with uncontrollable shakes…I begin to sob in a fit of joy.

24. Find The Will

Ruth

I stare at her front door until my eyes burn from lack of blinking. She's my best friend. The girl who shed a thousand tears for me after I was maimed and brutalized. The woman who held Dessin in her arms as he took his last breath.

I need to make this right.

There isn't much time.

Something wet nudges my elbow. I flinch.

DaiSzek chuffs next to me, bumping me again and again and again.

"Alright," I whisper-laugh. "I'll grow a pair."

My hand clenches into a fist, hovering over the oak door to knock and wake Skylenna. But before my hand meets the wood, the door flies open. She looks down at me with red, swollen eyes, dressed in her nightgown.

"Hey," I say awkwardly. "Can I come in?"

She nods, wiping her runny nose with the back of her hand.

I roll my chair through the entryway, following her into the bedroom. The one with Dessin's sleeping body.

"Are you okay?" I ask.

She sits on the reading chair next to his bed. Her sigh is sad and carries no sign of anger.

"Okay, I'll start." I rest my hands on my armrests. "I understand where you're coming from. Why you wouldn't want me to go back to that place. Especially…"

My eyes slide to Dessin's hands. "Especially after what you've lost."

Skylenna follows my gaze to his hand. She looks like she might burst into tears at any given moment.

"And I'm sorry for putting you in the position where you have to say goodbye to someone else. I am so sorry, Skylenna. From the bottom of my heart. You don't deserve to lose anyone else you love. I know your heart is hurting. I *know*."

My friend looks so broken. So defeated. It's almost enough to change my mind.

"But I need you to apologize to me now. It wasn't your intention to make me feel weak earlier. Of course, it wasn't. You would have said no to Warrose going. To Niles going. But I gave up my…ability to walk for my family. I'm suffering because of undying loyalty. For that, I am *strong*."

I can see it all over her face. How much my words are wounding her.

"And above all else, I deserve the right to be the decision-maker for my future. I deserve to call the shots for my own actions. I deserve to feel strong. I deserve to feel powerful!" I'm clutching the edges of my armrests as I tremble from the anger and determination that possess my soul.

Skylenna breaks down. "I'm so sorry! Yes! God, of course, you deserve all those things. I'd never doubt for a second that you aren't powerful. You're my best friend, I swear, I only want the best for you!"

In a single, terrible sob, Skylenna falls to the floor in front of me. Her face falls into my lap. "Forgive me, Ruth! The people of Vexamen would be lucky to have you. Forgive me for making you feel weak! But do not forgive me for anything else. I don't deserve it. I can't forgive myself for letting you get hurt in that prison. I was the *only* one who could have prevented it."

She's so frail. Her trembling arms drape around my waist, feeble and cold. And I cry with her, running my hand over her tangled hair, clutching that quivering frame to my body in an attempt to hold on to my best friend a little longer.

"I forgive you for everything, Skylenna." Our sobs make a healing symphony around us. "Please forgive yourself. It's what Kane and Dessin would have wanted. And one day, when they wake up…you'll feel strong again, too."

"Will I see you again?"

My heart crumbles at her words.

"Yes. I'll make it home for Sunday dinner as often as I can," I reply.

"Okay." Skylenna pulls me away to think for a moment. "You know, Dessin told me about a time when he was being trained by Demechnef that he felt so weak, he wasn't sure if he could overcome it. They were forcing his alters to switch, committing unspeakable acts of violence. And they started to provoke one of his most vicious alters—Dai."

I blink in surprise. "Dai…like *DaiSzek*?"

 She nods.

"It's an alter that was split off to, well." Skylenna rubs the back of her neck. "To tear an enemy apart in a grotesque, ferocious way. To leave their body unrecognizable. The way an attack from a real RottWeilen would look."

"Oh…" I try not to imagine it. But those images populate in my thoughts like a spreading fire.

"One day, Demechnef caught a pair of new subjects for him to kill. They chained them up in the hunting room, and when they let Dai loose, he refrained from killing him. Dessin didn't know what changed, he has no memory of why Dai refused, but instead, he murdered their trainers. Tore them to ribbons. The two subjects disappeared. And from that day on, Dessin started torturing his captors, one by one. He sought his revenge out so skillfully, they never even knew their demise was because of him."

"So you don't know why Dai decided to spare those subjects and attack his captors instead?" I ask.

Skylenna shakes her head. "No idea. The only bit of information

Dessin was able to pull from their gatekeeper alter, Cricket, was that something those subjects said or did gave Dai the will to turn his vehemence on those who deserved it."

I look down at Dessin's sleeping face in awe. What an incredible human being. So complex. So magnificent.

"My point is that if all those alters were able to find their strength through a dark and terrifying environment like that, then you will make a fierce and formidable queen to the Vexamen people, Ruth." She holds my hands as her voice wavers. "I believe in you."

"For the alters," I announce proudly.

"For the alters."

25. The Black Knight

Ruth

Warrose waits for me under a stream of moonlight.

The harvest ball has cleared out. No more music or dancers. No more tables of feasts and drinks. Only Warrose sitting on a bale of hay in front of a dying bonfire.

"How did it go?" he asks without looking up.

I wipe my eyes of residual tears and sniffle but give him no answer.

He straightens that hulking back, glancing back at me with narrowing eyes. Suspicion. Concern. Slight alarm.

"That's it then…" he muses, studying the tracks of tears on my cheeks in the light of the silver moon. "You've made your decision."

It wasn't one I had to put a lot of thought into here. Since the axe, I have been begging God for purpose, praying for a reason to persevere past the pain and trauma.

That reason walked into the ball tonight and kneeled at my feet.

"Yes," I say, the urge to cry still lacing my voice.

"You told Skylenna?" He turns to face me.

"I think she knew the moment they asked me."

His bright sea water irises drop to the yellow leaves littering the ground under his feet. He nods a few times slowly.

"It might be stupid, and I might get myself killed…" I blurt out.

Warrose lifts his chin. It's hard to tell in this light, but I think the corner of his mouth is lifting.

"Oh?" he says.

"I don't know what I'm doing…" I continue.

He watches me without blinking.

"And I don't want you to feel obligated or anything…"

"Go on."

"But…" I scratch my head nervously. "You wanna…you know…"

Those corners pull up just a little bit more. "No, I don't know. You're going to have to ask me in a complete sentence, little rebel."

My arms are made of melting putty, my thighs are throbbing, and I can already feel a hangover spurring onyet my body is buzzing with adrenaline.

"Do you want to go to Vexamen with me? Help me take the throne? Help me stop the Meat Carnivals?" My gulp is heard from all corners of this forest. I cross my arms to try and appear more confident, but it only makes him smile wider.

"That's a hell of a lot of time we'll be committing to spending together…"

Doubt curdles in my gut, but I don't let it show on my face.

"…especially for someone who couldn't stand me a few months ago," he adds.

"Yeah, so?"

He quirks a gorgeous smile. "So, are you saying you'd like to go on epic adventures with me?"

"Well, I don't know if I'd put it that way—"

"And be the only two people we can trust in a country full of conspirators and sick individuals who won't support your claim?"

"Yes."

"Spend large amounts of time in close quarters where we'll talk for hours?" Warrose grows significantly more serious.

I nod.

He watches me without blinking. "Why me?"

"I trust you." It's a stupid question. Why not him?

"You trust Helga Bee and Gerta too. Why *me*?"

"You're really going to be a smart aleck bastard about this, aren't you?" I grit.

"Yes, I am," he says.

I huff. "Because! You've stuck by my side more than anyone. You've carried the weight of my anger and grief and proven you're strong enough to handle me at my worst. I can do this on my own, but why would I want to? You're the man I want to do it with."

Warrose ties his hair back away from his face, thinking deeply on how he wants to respond.

"There's this story I heard of an Alkadonian queen. She was born in a forest, raised by the animals. When she decided to claim the throne after finding out she was the next rightful heir, no one stood with her." He stands to his full towering height. "Except a black knight who saw she led with an army of animals at her back. He stood by her throne until the day she died."

I blink up at him, wondering if this means what I think it means...

"Fuck yes, I'll go with you." Lowering himself to one knee, he kisses my hand. "I'll be your black knight, and we'll arrive with an army of beasts at our backs."

26. The Group Hug

Ruth

No sleep.

All night packing, planning, coordinating. Asena, Runa, and a few others arrived to go over the map, to explain the different animals that would support a ruler to liberate them.

We meet Helga Bee and Gerta on the beach, followed by a small legion of animals that the colonies have gathered and gently tamed over the series for this purpose. Following me into a country of animal cruelty to claim their throne. Fighting in a war has been seeping through their veins since birth. And Warrose knows nearly all of them by name.

Among them are the Winter Storm Lions.

Our friends from the East Vexello Mountains begin loading our personal belongings as my friends gather on the shore to…

Say goodbye.

For now.

The sun blasts through the briny sky, singeing through the sea mist, warming our skin as Warrose and I sigh as Chekiss is the last to arrive.

"We should all be going with you," Niles argues, arms crossed and frowning down at me.

"No!" Warrose and I say together.

"Marilynn has obligations here. To make this a better place for women. For *children*," I say, squeezing her hand. "And…Dessin is *here*."

A great pain I'll never know swallows Skylenna's gaze whole. She's absent in that complex mind for a moment. This beach. Her memories. The void. Though her abilities are an unknown to all of us, it isn't hard to see that she's reliving a death as her feet sink into this sand.

"But there's something *you* can do for me before we leave," I direct to Marilynn.

She hooks a straight piece of radiant ruby hair behind her ear and nods, as if she knows exactly what I'm going to ask.

"I know you're not allowed to tell us anything of the future. I know. But we're family. And I need you to tell me this one thing." I move closer. "Is this…is this a suicide mission?"

Her all-knowing ocean eyes dig into my soul. "Would that stop you from going?"

I glance up at Warrose, who has the same look of vicious determination on his chiseled face as I feel in my heart.

"No, it would not."

Niles makes a whiny sound and kicks the sand.

"It isn't a suicide mission, Ruth. You will be extraordinary." Her eyes rise to the big man standing behind me. "You both will."

My lungs deflate as I sag in relief, releasing the anxious hold on my armrests. No matter what, it's my purpose now to do this. I have something to drive me through the pain, the nightmares, the flashbacks, the phantom itches on my ankles. The vivid mental image of the axe that won't go away.

"Come here, child." Chekiss leans down to grab my face and place a soft kiss on my forehead. He smells like the pipe and pumpernickel.

Marilynn hugs me next, whispering that her child will only know Vexamen to be a great country with an even greater leader.

Niles stands before me, looking almost angry.

"It's a short ride on the ship. I'm going to come home as often as I can for Sunday dinners," I reassure him.

His nostrils flare. "You promise?"

"I promise, buddy."

He moves to me slowly, like if he takes his time, that will prolong the inevitable. Delay my departure. I laugh, holding out my arms for him.

"And you'll keep in touch?" he asks before embracing me.

"Yes."

"Send letters by pigeon?"

I laugh. "Sure!"

"Send me souvenirs?"

I roll my eyes and grin up at him.

"I'm going to miss you like hell, little Ruthie." His face softens, moisture gathering in his eyes. "You're my best friend."

"I already miss you, Niles!"

Our hug lingers as the bustling winds of the ocean whip around us.

DaiSzek and Skylenna kneel to my side next, she holds my hands with her cold, clammy skin. Those eyes sunken in tired circles.

"Dessin would be so proud of you," she says, unable to look me in the eye. "*I'm* so proud of you."

"Hey." I lift her chin. "He would have tried to stop me from going too."

She chuckles. "He was the most stubborn out of all of us."

"*Is*," I correct.

Something like shame morphs in her eyes.

"Skylenna?"

Those glowing emerald eyes lift to meet mine.

"He's coming back. That coma is nothing compared to the sheer will and fight he still has in him." I wipe her tears, but they keep coming. "Until then…you're going to take care of his baby, okay? And you're going to take care of yourself. That's what he would want."

The following hug she throws around my body is full of pain and pride, drenched in an ache only one man can soothe. One. Man.

"I love you so much. You'll always be my sister, Ruth," she sobs quietly into my shoulder.

"I love you more."

After a few moments, the group gathers around me as if on instinct. No one needs the request to do this anymore like we used to. The group hug happens without any words at all.

Even DaiSzek nuzzles his nose between us to join in.

We're only missing one person now.

27. The Abyss Looks Back

Ruth

As the sun drops to nothing but a glimmery hot coal over the Midnight Sea horizon, I remain in my spot port side.

Warrose went to bed an hour ago, though it was still light. He claimed to have motion sickness from the waves. I laughed at him as Helga Bee guided him to his own room.

Not *our* room.

The insecure part of me wonders if he requested it that way.

But I shake my head and stare off into the amber-lit abyss. I have to focus on what's to come. The laws and changes I'd like to make. I've been studying every book Marilynn could find about Vexamen history, their laws, rules, and culture.

The biggest one I'll be tackling is the inhumane Meat Carnival. Reading about it on this boat has turned my stomach sour. The photographs. The drawings. The vivid, horrible descriptions are too much to bear. How could anyone be this cruel? How could no one have a heart when looking at these wonderful beasts.

Head Beastkeeper begins the carnival by torturing the animals, believing fear and adrenaline will enhance the taste of the meat.

Animals shall hang on display—still alive—for hours, or in some cases days before they finally die.

Tears gather in my eyes at the thought of witnessing such acts in person.

The idea makes me murderous. It makes me want to sentence all of them to Warrose's wrath. He loves animals even more than I do. I wonder if he knows these fine details, too.

I watch the gentle Winter Storm Lions sleep on the bow of the ship, play, and eat the food we've brought for them. A few other creatures make themselves at home too.

I don't know how I got this lucky to receive such support.

"Are you afraid, little rebel?"

That gravelly, baritone voice. The ability it has to tighten every muscle in my body.

I don't turn to him. I don't take my eyes off that gorgeous horizon and sensational ocean breeze. I merely shrug a shoulder and smile to myself.

"No, I don't think so." *Yes. Most definitely.*

"And why not?" He's standing right behind me now. That monstrous shadow engulfing my presence whole.

I glance back at him, then up, up, up, dazzled by the way his hazel eyes catch fire in the dimming sunset.

"Because I have my black knight. Who can hurt me?"

His dark eyebrows turn upward as his stance seems to soften at the sentiment of my words. His lips part in partial surprise.

I'm caught off guard as my eyes falter to his bare chest. The raised tattoos on his arms. The subtle outline of each individual muscle across his tightly coiled abs. Without his shirt, the black pants hug his hips nicely, revealing the start of that V.

"That's right," he finally says.

I return my eyes back to his face, flushing with a small burst of embarrassment.

He's...so nice to look at.

"Do you want to go over the plan again?" I ask.

Warrose blinks.

"For how we'll take down those in rebellion…" I add with narrowing eyes.

"Did you mean what you said at the harvest ball?" Those eyes burn straight through my skin. I squirm under that hazel fire.

What do I say? His face is unreadable. There are no clear signs with his body language.

I shrug casually. "Of course not. I was drunk."

He scoffs, looking away to the glorious sunset about to fade away in a blink.

"Oh hell no." He pinches the bridge of his nose. "We're not still doing this. You are so goddamned stubborn."

I open my mouth to object, but he swoops down to capture my lips with his roughly, bruising my mouth with a vicious attempt to show me something. To peel past my own stubbornness. The kiss sends a jolt of tingling warmth straight through my jaw, down down down into my belly.

"I'm yours." He pants against my lips. "*Yours!* Do you understand? Does that get past your stubborn-ass, thick-ass skull? I'm the one who's not good enough to be with you. I know that. But I'm going to put in the work every fucking day."

The bottom half of my face trembles as if it can't decide if it wants to grin or cry.

"I'll be your punching bag when you're hurting and need to hurt something. I'll argue when you're being a little know-it-all-asshole. But what I'm *not* going to keep doing is this same old song and dance. This game was fun in the beginning. But now it just hurts. I no longer wish to pretend like I don't lose my breath when you enter the room. Do you see this?" He grabs my hand, placing it over his bare chest. His *heart.* "This! This is where it burns and twists and aches to not be able to hold you. To kiss you. To love you. Do you want to be with me, Ruth?"

I part my lips to answer.

"Be with me as in kiss me in the mornings and make love to me at night? Tell me all of your secrets and let me protect your heart?" he clarifies.

I finally let that niggle of hope creep into my mind. That string of want and desire that I've been suppressing since the prison took everything from me. Since I stopped believing that I could ever have

Warrose's heart. I picture it all. Making love every night. Finally telling him how much he means to me. Governing an unlawful country together. Kisses during breakfast. Telling him how much I love him.

"Yes," I whisper.

His back straightens. "And you're sober when you say this?"

"I'm completely sober." The start of a rare smile blooms across my cheeks.

"Then say it," he commands.

I breathe in the ocean's mist, salty air, and his subtle scent of a campfire.

"You let me fall to pieces when we finally got to a safe place just like you promised. And when you couldn't put those pieces back together, you mixed your pieces with my own. You *joined* me in the dark." I hold his face in between my small hands. "I can't promise to always be a ray of sunshine like Niles, but that when I do have good days, you'll always be a part of them. You became my rock in that prison. You made me believe it was worth staying alive when all I wanted was for that axe to finish the job!"

Warrose's become red and watery, and it nearly rips my heart out.

"I want to be with you. I want to be with you. I want"

He doesn't let me finish. In a swift, fluid motion, Warrose hooks his hands around my waist, and lifts me to sit on the edge of the ship's railing. Those wide hands firmly support my back as the sea winds whip against me.

It's the first time I'm almost eye level with him without Warrose having to kneel.

Even as he reclines me backward and kisses my neck like a hungry lion feeding on prey, I'm not afraid he'll drop me. I let my head fall back and gaze into the abyss of the night sky, now beautifully mixed with the sparkling ocean.

"I'm sorry…" Warrose curses under his breath. "I swear I'm going to spend time worshipping you. I'm going to take my time. But I have to have you now. Is that okay?"

I run my hand through his hair as I savor the taste of him on my lips. I nod, but a traitorous thought pushes deep into the back of my mind.

"Can you…do you think you can get…*hard?*"

Warrose blinks rapidly and cocks his head back in shock. He looks offended.

"Pardon?"

"Well, I mean, it's okay if not…"

Where has my confidence gone?

"For Christ's sake, Ruth." He traps my hand in his own, then drags it up the hard length of his crotch.

No words come out of my mouth as my jaw falls open. I look up at him in temporary astonishment. I guess I've forgotten how big he is. Flashbacks pour into my mind from the Mazonist dinner party.

Heat blasts between my legs in volcanic proportions.

"I see."

"I'm hard every time I see you. Every time you're near. It's bad for my fucking circulation." Warrose breathes heavily. His lids are lowered and hazy, as if he's drunk.

I add a little more pressure, and we groan at the fiery electricity buzzing from the contact. My pussy slickens at the gravelly noise his throat makes when he's turned on.

"Spread your legs," he orders in a hushed voice.

My eyes dart around to the dark, empty deck of the ship.

"What if someone sees us?" I ask.

"That didn't seem to bother us in the prison." He levels his hazel eyes on me. "I promise to stay vigilant."

A breathy laugh escapes me, but I do as he says. My pinched thighs part slowly, allowing those big hands to slide over my chilled skin, hiking up my dress. The breeze is mixed with his hot breath on my sensitive flesh as he leans in. Thumbs caressing my inner thighs as he stays quiet for a moment.

This is the first time I'm going to be intimate with someone in my new reality. My changed body. And I'm finally ready. Scared, yes, but ready. The thoughts pour into my head of what he'll think when he sees me naked. Will he be disappointed because he's always pictured me naked differently? Will he love what he sees no matter what?

"You have a gorgeous cunt, Ruth."

I can't help but smile and lose my breath at the twinkling midnight sky.

"Do you think you can take my fingers?" He runs the pad of his thumb over my throbbing clit.

I bare down my teeth at the debilitating pleasure that overtakes my senses.

God, his fingers…they're long and thick. Can I handle them? I must.

He inches his index finger inside me slowly. "Hold still."

My body quivers in the wind, still hovering over the edge of the ship. I fight the urge not to buck or squirm as his finger pushes through to the hilt.

"That feels nice, doesn't it?" His husky voice is dark and thoroughly pleased.

"Mmm," I answer.

As his index finger hooks inside my warmth, his thumb kneads and massages my swollen clit. The back and forth is steady and methodical. My breath enters and exits in damn near violent bursts of energy.

I've never had a man touch me like this. Not ever. The last was a loser. A dud that had no idea how to navigate the female anatomy. But *this* man seems to be genuinely fascinated by the way I clench and unclench around his knuckle. The rhythm to which my body moves and reacts to him.

Warrose presses his forehead to mine, trapping our breath together, our eagerness and agony to mate again and again and again. His finger pumps in a gentle, seductive motion, eliciting as much wetness as I can produce.

"Oh my god!" I grunt as an orgasm sneaks up on me, creeping forward with ease.

"No, don't come yet." He kisses me twice. "I want to feel you do that around my cock, yes?"

"Yes!"

Now. I want him so bad. I want to know what it feels like to be his in every way. Is this what I wanted since those early days when we were trapped in that prison? Maybe even before then?

With one hand still holding my lower back, he unhooks his belt, dropping his pants low enough to release his large erection.

"*Wow.*" I make a face at my outburst.

Warrose studies my expression, watching me as I take in the massiveness of his dick.

"What?" he says.

"It's…big."

He narrows his eyes thoughtfully. "Put your hands around it for me."

A shiver travels up my spine. My hands stack on top of each other as I wrap my fingers around him. He's warm and firm like a rock, slightly twitching within my grip.

"Fuck." Warrose lets his head fall back. "Those pretty hands are so small, aren't they?"

They sure as hell are. They aren't even close to being big enough to cover his shaft completely. My palms tingle with pleasure radiating up my elbows and into my bloodstream.

"Warrose," I exhale, something close to a whine.

"I know." His eyes are wild, frenzied with lust and an animalistic desire.

I spread my legs wider, inviting him to feel me on the inside. Inviting him to take me. To make love to me. To have me always.

And before he does anything of that nature, his two fingers spread my lips, and he just stares at my center with parted lips.

"I'm not going to be able to sleep tonight until you let me lick your cunt clean of all your cum. Will you indulge me in that?"

My pussy quivers open and closed at the thought of him licking me softly, in no rush, for his own pleasure of tasting me.

The head of his cock nudges my entrance, using my natural lubrication to work himself in the first inch. He clenches his jaw and releases a loud breath through his nose.

"*Ow*." I wince. No way this is already hurting. I'm not a virgin! Is it his size? Has it been that long since the last time I laid with someone?

"I'll go slow."

Please.

He waits, stroking my hair away from my face, taking in the way my mouth stays open as I try to adjust and let my body relax.

"I was moments away from laying you down on that dining table and taking you in front of our friends and the Mazonist Brothers at the prison," he reminisces, barely holding it together.

"You were?"

"It would have taken three seconds with your mouth around my cock for me to end it all there. I didn't care who watched. I wanted you so goddamned bad."

My inner walls start to loosen.

"Fuck, Ruth, I wanted to fuck you until it blinded me."

His husky words cause me to flush with hot wetness. He slips in another inch without any effort at all.

I latch onto his neck, moaning against his mouth. *"More!"*

The tendons in his large neck go tight. He holds me against the taut planes of his body, unable to relax as my opening flutters around his girth. That dominance pouring off him is subtle, yet I still drown in it.

"Spread the lips of your cunt for me again," he commands darkly. "I can't wait any longer."

Neither can I.

There's no room for insecurity as I use my index and middle finger to pull apart my lips and expose the shiny pink flesh for him to gaze down at.

His deep groan sounds like a growl.

"I'm going to paint your clit in my cum."

With a final, gentle push, he's inside me. All the way. I'm momentarily paralyzed. Filled to the brim. Gasping for air. Unable to move or adjust.

He saws out of me, then back in again.

The motion has me swaying backward, arching my back to the sky and bending backward toward the ocean waves slapping against the ship.

"Fuck," he hisses, yanking me back against his chest. "Don't do that again!"

Rebellion crackles like lightning in my chest. "Yes, *Daddy.*"

Warrose growls, and the sound is simply euphoric to my ears. Flames kiss my inner thighs. Dizziness swells behind my eyes.

"And don't fucking call me that." He pumps in me again. His cock now fully coated with my wetness.

The fire in his eyes to keep me submissive is beautiful. However, I can't help but push him a little further. Just to see what he'll do. My inner walls clench around his heavy erection with a worshipful grip.

His reaction is small, hardly noticeable. I watch those gleaming eyes close slowly, and his teeth grit together.

"Please," I whisper. He already has me addicted to this.

"What do you need, baby girl?" His cock works in and out of me at a devilishly seductive pace. So slow. So strategic.

"Please, *Daddy*. I need to come."

Warrose snatches my mouth with his own and growls into our kiss as if that *name* fills him with rage. Yet his dick pulsates and grows much harder at my plea.

"How about this?" he asks, running a rough, calloused thumb along my glistening clit.

"Yes," I exhale, gulping down the excitement buzzing through my veins. "Yes, Daddy."

That hoarse growl rumbles up his throat again. Those hazel irises appear absolutely feral. Wild. Incoherent. He leans down to clamp his teeth down on my shoulder.

Despite the ache, I let out a panicked moan. Loud, frantic, and impossible that it isn't waking the whole ship up. The electric charge of his rutting motions deep inside me passes through my entire nervous system, forcing a forking tremble to snake up my arms and back.

I'm so close.

Is he really going to make me come on the edge of a ship?

It builds, builds, builds until the wave of pleasure dwarfs us completely. I'm speechless. Watching bursts of white blind my vision.

"Oh... *Oh!*" It's all I can say to warn him.

He unlatches his teeth from my shoulder. "You going to get my dick nice and wet with your cum?"

I nod, pant, nod again. The orgasm gathers in my lower belly like a storm forming on the horizon.

Warrose eats up the way my expression tightens and pinches together as I brace for something to snap inside of me.

He exhales through his nose before he speaks. "Doesn't it feel good when *Daddy* fucks you like this?"

Heat blasts up my spine as I come, squeezing the life out of his arms to ground me through the climax. I contract around his girth in beautiful pulses of lasting ecstasy. My molars grind against each other as I groan to the sky.

"*Oh god!*" I howl.

He ruts inside me carelessly, erotically.

"Fuck, I can't hold it in after that."

Those thrusts become violent, uncivilized, and nearly throwing me off the edge of the ship.

I'll want you for the rest of my life.

Warrose grunts against my lips like an animal. Savage and brutal as he pulls out of my soaking channel, spilling his hot seed across my pelvic bone, clit, and dripping down between my cheeks.

As we let the tides rest, I wrap my arms around his neck and clutch him to my weak, fragile frame. The ocean breeze is chilly, carrying a fine, salty mist that raises goose bumps on my skin. But as I bury my face in the crook of his neck, I know that he will always be my warmth. My solid wall of stone to lean against.

Constant.

Formidable.

Never leaving my side.

"Little rebel?" he murmurs against my cold cheek.

"Hmm?"

"That song we've been dancing to is over now. Can I hold you for good now?"

But what I'm not going to keep doing is this same old song and dance. This game was fun in the beginning. But now it just hurts. I no longer wish to pretend like I don't lose my breath when you enter the room.

I don't sob or wail at the lovely intent of his words. Warm tears line my eyes like a second skin. And I smile at the stars that watch us hold each other among the crashing waves and glittering water. Because it's finally over. The dance of pretending not to notice when my whole world spins as he walks into a room. It's finally over.

"No more dancing," I whisper with fresh tears. "We're finally home."

28. Prince Prophesied

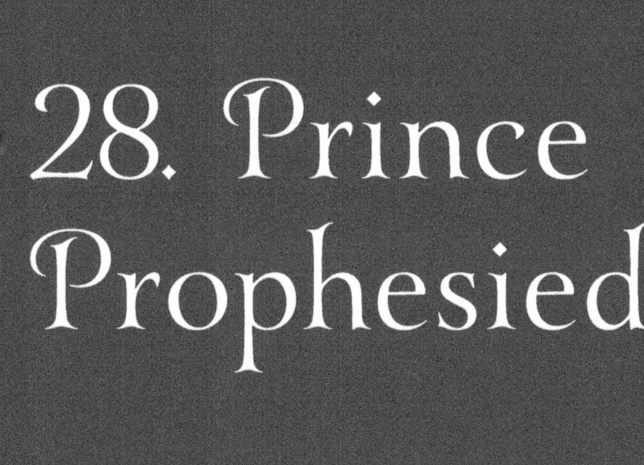

Marilynn

Six Months Later

The crying stops abruptly as the midwife places the precious baby boy in Niles's arms.

The room goes still. Not a single sound as he stares down at the newborn without blinking. One moment, two, three…

Niles sobs in complete silence.

And I cry too, letting him have a moment before he passes my baby boy to me.

"I'm going to love you as much as my father loved me, little boy. I promise."

I cry harder.

"And I promise to do right by the father who couldn't be here. I'll always protect you," he whispers, breathing in the scent of the baby's head.

"Niles," I finally call, my voice hoarse from pure exhaustion.

"Okay. Time to meet your beautiful mommy." Those tan hands pass my baby boy over, laying him on my chest, and pressed to my face.

The tears don't stop falling as I'm practically blinded by a new love I've never felt before. I'm suddenly scared, overwhelmed, joyous, overprotective, and giddy all at once.

My son.

My baby boy.

I can't believe he's finally here. A pair of tired, confused ocean-blue eyes blink up at me before closing in pure exhaustion.

"He's so handsome, sweetheart," Niles says, kissing my forehead.

"He is."

We watch him coo and snuggle for a long time as my midwife cleans up the bedroom. Knowing full well, Chekiss, Skylenna, DaiSzek, Ruth, and Warrose are all waiting in the hallway, beaming with excitement to meet him.

After these last few months with Niles taking care of me, feeding my cravings in the dead of night, rubbing my sore feet, rubbing oil on my round belly—I've fallen even more in love with him. Going against every effort to not love him, to not like him, to not get to know him.

Loving Niles was inevitable.

I've come to accept my own defeat.

I've come to cherish that God has given me the most loving, loyal, and purest soul in the world. There's no going back now.

"I knew he was going to be a little boy too, ya know?" Niles comments sleepily.

"Oh?" I raise an eyebrow. "And it has nothing to do with the fact that I've been saying he's going to be a boy per the prophecy or anything."

"Mmm, don't interrupt, 'kay?"

I laugh and nod for him to continue.

"I had a dream about you a few weeks ago. You—" Niles shakes his head as if trying to rid himself of a wicked thought. "You died in my arms."

I straighten from my slouched position.

"I, what?"

"You were an old woman. Still so beautiful. I could tell it was you from those big beautiful blue eyes." He smiles down at the baby boy in my arms. "And you said '*I know I could have left this world holding my son's hands… But I need the last face I see to be yours, Niles. I need to die in the arms of my soulmate.*'"

It's only a dream, yet my heart stings.

"Why didn't you tell me about this dream?" I ask tightly.

He shakes his head again and sighs. "Because it bothered me for days. Left a knot in my stomach. The thought of you leaving me alone in this world is mortifying to me. You can't leave me, okay?"

I kiss him softly, praying those dark thoughts away. "I love you, my sweet Niles."

"I love you too. Gah, I'm sorry. This isn't really a topic for such a day of celebration. Is it?" Niles wiggles his pinkie that is being held captive by my newborn's hand. "Are you going to tell me his name now?"

I smile. Kissing baby boy on his soft head with a light dusting of black hair.

"This has been his name since I was a little girl. The man who one day will change *everything*." I sigh, remembering how I always swore to myself I would change the name to defy the prophecy. Not because this name holds significant meaning, but because this name has already made its way through history that dates back long before I was born. But now, I can't wait to watch this all unfold. I can't wait to see this baby boy turn into the man who has made his mark through time.

"I'd like you to meet, Niklaus Demechnef."

29. "I've seen it all."

Ruth

1 Year Later

We're both roaring drunk as Warrose licks me viciously while I'm perched on my throne.

It's the third time today.

I grip his hair until I'm sure his scalp screams in pain, but the added suction to my clit is throwing me over the cliff. I moan like a madwoman in the throne room, grinding against his tongue to chase the climax to the end.

"Fuck," he growls against my throbbing cunt.

"You just can't get enough, can you?" I tease, pulling down my dress.

I grab the handlebars of my moving chair and lift myself over from my throne seat to that one. And despite all the money we now have, I'll never get another mobile chair. This one is special. It can never be replaced. The love of my life made it for me.

The motion of shifting to a new spot has my head rolling around. The throne room shifts, and I sway with it.

"Whoa. Have we really drunk that much?" His big, calloused hands steady me.

I just grin up at him stupidly.

"That's a yes." He laughs, kissing me all over my face.

"We're celebrating!"

The horrendous and gut-wrenching Meat Carnival arena has been officially abolished and rebuilt into a rehabilitation orphanage for the children who were being trained to be in the Vexamen Breed. It's also a sanctuary for the beasts wounded in battle (those that aren't dangerous). Warrose and I are so proud of the work we've done. So proud of our perseverance to change the worst things about this place.

When we arrived to claim my rights as a Mazonist ruler, to my surprise, I already had a large following of supporters. The East Vexello Mountaineers, the prisoners that were set free who were wrongfully convicted, and a large population of the villagers. After the abused beasts of this country saw what I was doing and witnessed the Winter Storm Lions lining up to defend me—the mistreated and misunderstood creatures rallied on my side as well.

Although…we didn't even have to free them from their cages. Warrose said they were freed before we even escaped the prison. Many extremists were trying to hunt them all down and throw them back in their cages, with little success. But regardless, the majority were freed.

No one has stepped forward to claim that liberation.

We may never know who it was.

"Yes, we are! Drink as much as you want! But first, I'm getting us dinner on the balcony to overlook the sanctuary." Another kiss on my lips this time. "Yes?"

"Yes!" I thrust my fist in the air. "Food. Good. Yum."

His chuckle is mesmerizing, making my pussy fill with heat again.

As he runs off, I'm left alone for a few long moments. Gazing out drunkenly to my throne room, I announce a confession.

"I don't know if I'll be a good ruler, but I'll always try my best. No matter how bad the nightmares get. I'll always try my best." I nod through the vicious spins.

"Your best is more than enough," a young, feminine voice calls out from the shadows.

My drunk brain freezes up. "Who's over there?"

Rolling my chair forward, I tap the crossbow strapped to the back of my chair.

"Someone who loves you dearly," the woman's voice says softly.

She steps out from the shadows, wearing a crimson cloak and hood. The shadows cover most of her face, yet I can make out her eyes. Heterochromatic eyes. One chocolate brown. One emerald green. A stunning, very familiar face.

"Who are you?" I utter.

"I grew up never appreciating what you've done here. In this country. It's the cost of being so privileged," she says. Voice familiar too. Who does it remind me of? "Not until I had to live through the horrors you worked so hard to abolish. I never knew..."

The woman lowers her head somberly.

"And I never really understood what you did for my parents either."

"Who are your parents?" God, why am I so deliriously drunk for this conversation?

The woman only smiles, eyes growing glossy.

"Anyway, I only came to give you some reassurance. It's the least I can do now," she tells me, reaching for my hand.

"What's that?"

"You're going to be the greatest ruler in history. More than any Alkadonian. More than anyone in our timeline."

I grip the armrests of my seat to keep from spinning even more. To keep from vomiting.

"How could..." Nausea blasts through my gut. "How could you know that?"

The woman kneels before me with tears streaming down her cheeks.

"Because I've already seen it come to pass."

Epilogue
"Your Father Was a Great Man..."

Seven Years Later

Sapphire S Valdawell

They said his eyes were a beautiful, rich shade of brown…
But I've never seen them.

They are always closed. Not awake. Not here. Sleeping. Dreaming. *Dead.*

I stand over my father's comatose body in a white nightgown with clenched fists and tear-streaked cheeks.

After another nightmare of chasing him through the white halls of the Emerald Lake Asylum, I cried in my bed for an hour before walking into this room. He kept running from me. Didn't turn around to see me reach for his hand. Didn't care to hear my small voice scream "Daddy!"

My father, the infamous Patient Thirteen, kept running.

I never come in here. Only Mom, Krimson, and DaiSzek. Every time I walk past this room, I'm filled with hatred and fury. Why won't he wake up for me? It's not hard to open your eyes. It's easy! *Wake up! Don't you want to meet me? They said you were powerful! Am I not enough?*

But then I wonder…what if he needs help? Have I let him down?

"I hate you…" I whisper under my breath, watching the shadows from the fireplace darken my father's face. His sunken cheeks. His pointed nose. That pale skin.

"That's a shame because I know how much he loves you."

I jump, spinning around to see Uncle Warrose's gigantic frame taking up the doorway. My small body relaxes, and I turn back to face my father.

"He doesn't even know me," I reply, wiping my tears in shame.

"You don't really believe that, do you?" he asks.

I shrug. Is he stupid or something? My father is basically dead.

"After everything you've heard of his power? His great mind? You really don't think he already knows you and loves you so much, little Sapphire?"

I shake my head.

Those are just stories.

If he was so great and powerful, he wouldn't be lying in a bed like this.

"What's really on your mind?" Uncle Warrose places a heavy hand on my small shoulder.

I consider running out of the room and hiding under my blankets, maybe climbing into bed with my brother, or snuggling DaiSzek…but the nightmare will still be there when I close my eyes again.

I look up at my uncle and say with watering eyes, "I can't save him."

He raises his thick, dark eyebrows. "Why do you say that?"

"Because I'm seven." My blurry eyes find the man in the bed again, trying to ignore the vast ache in my chest at the sight of him. "I'm not like him. There's nothing special about me."

Uncle Warrose grunts, taking a knee in his dull midnight armor and belt of shiny weapons clanking together. He spins me to face him.

"You're seven. It may look like that now as a child, but I know something you don't as your father's best friend. Do you want to know what it is?"

Tears drip down my hot cheeks as I nod.

"Your father could move heaven and hell to get what he wanted, to save those he loved. He'd find a way to turn back the clock if he really wanted to."

"Really?" The deep, echoing ache in my lungs grows hopeful and light.

"Yes. But here's the thing…you not only have his blood, but your mother's as well."

"What's that mean?"

His hazel eyes bore into me. "It means, your father may have been a great man…but my darling, you will be *astounding.*"

To be continued in the fifth and final installment of The Pawn and The Puppet series:
The Clock and The Carnival

Acknowledgments

I am both excited and dreading writing the book that comes after this one, *The Clock and The Carnival.* Since I was fifteen years old, I've dreamt of the characters and vivid detail, I've built their stories brick by brick. And when I published the first book in 2022, it was a dream come true to watch this story, this world become real for all of you too. I love Skylenna, Kane, Dessin, and DaiSzek so much. Thank you for loving them as much as me, if not more. I promise, even though things look grim right now with their story, I promise the ending will not disappoint. In the next and last book of *The Pawn and The Puppet* series, the events to come will blow you away. You can count on that.

As always, thank you to my mom! To this day, she remains the only soul to know every detail of how this story goes and ends. Her excitement, tears, and passion for my work gives me endless inspiration. I love you, Mom!

During my time writing this book, I've gotten pregnant, and want to thank my older sister, Lacey, for doing everything to take care of me during this time. She's been the sweetest support and light during a scary and thrilling chapter in my life.

Thank you to my cover designer, Stefanie Saw—you blow me away every time with your art. To my format designer, Amy Kessler—you work around the clock for every detail change I need, thank you for being superwoman! And to my editors, Ellie, Debbie, and Christine—you've been with me since day one of publishing, and I'm so thankful for all your hard work!

To my perfect beta readers: Danielle Caballero, Kayla Watson, Laura Pena, Ciera Sanchez, and my superb sensitivity readers Claudia De Chiara, Cassidy Marshall, and Mia Brandshaug (who has been my #1 cheerleader since day one)! Don't forget to check out the Instagram page she runs @thepawnandthepuppet!

About the Author

Brandi Elise Szeker has had a million stories in her head since she was a little girl convincing her baby sister there were killer clowns in the trees that came out after dark. She has four rescue dogs, Louis, Cali, Stella, and Nova. You can find them sprinkled throughout the series so that her love for them will live on forever. And some days, she lies awake at night wondering if she writes the most beautiful love stories, maybe one will find her too. Texas is where she currently resides, but one day, she'll be deep in the mountains, under the stars, writing a thousand more books that will both break your heart and give you life.

To learn more about Brandi, visit her at:
Author website & newsletter:
www.brandibookthought.com
TikTok & Instagram:
@brandibookthought
Author Facebook Page:
https://www.facebook.com/brandieliseszeker/
Spoilers Facebook Group for TP&TP:
www.facebook.com/groups/thepawnandthepuppetspoilers/